A BELINDA LAWRENCE MYSTERY

ILLUSION OF DEATH

BRIAN KAVANAGH

Copyright © 2018 Brian Kavanagh

Published by Vivid Publishing
A division of the Fontaine Publishing Group
P.O. Box 948 Fremantle
Western Australia 6959
www.vividpublishing.com.au

National Library of Australia Cataloguing-in-Publication data:
Author: Kavanagh, Brian, 1935-, author.
Title: Illusion of Death / Brian Kavanagh.
ISBN: 978-1-925846-43-0 (paperback)
Series: Belinda Lawrence mystery.
Dewey Number: A823.4

To discover more Brian Kavanagh books, to contact the author, please visit
www.vividpublishing.com.au/briankavanagh for further information.

With love for Lucy, Paul, Rae, Tom, Brian, Karen, Helen, Bob, Adele, Peter, Daniel, Grace, Susan, Phil, Lily.

"After a good dinner one can forgive anybody, even one's own relations."– Oscar Wilde

ABOUT THE AUTHOR

Producer/Director/Editor/Writer

With many years experience in film production Brian Kavanagh's career covers the areas of Production, Direction, Editing and Writing on features and documentaries.

Kavanagh is an accredited member of the Australian Screen Editors (A.S.E) by which he was honoured with a Lifetime Achievement Award in 1997 for his contribution to film making in Australia.

He is also a member of the Australian Society of Authors (A.S.A.).

Curtain Raiser

Max struggled against the ropes binding him. He was weak from hunger. It was cold on the floor, and his legs were numb, the cords were cutting off his blood supply. He had drifted in and out of consciousness and wondered how long he had been there.

One day? Three days?

A heavy bruise on his chest from the thrashing was aching, and his mouth was dry. If he could only remove the tape from his mouth and head to call for help. There must be someone to hear him.

The sound of footsteps in the hall alarmed him. He wondered who it would be this time.

Were they coming to beat him again?

Please. No more!

With terrified eyes he waited; watched as the door handle turned. The door was flung open as though to flaunt the supremacy of the new arrival.

It was an armed jailer.

Even in his terror, Max saw the irony in the choice of weapon.

Chapter One

The whip whistled through the air. Bit into human flesh. Blood began to flow.

Bridie Kelly stifled a yawn. She glanced at her watch. Not too long, now. Her gaze shifted to the others watching the flogging.

Harry Winters, on the edge of his seat, was watching keenly, eyes wide, mouth agape. Bridie couldn't be sure, but she thought he was drooling.

Joe O'Brien's grey head sagged to the side. He snored softly. Muriel, his wife, was away, so he was by himself tonight. Muriel wasn't that keen, and she often made excuses. Pity really, as she usually brought a cream sponge and once, some splendid Lamingtons. To Bridie's mind they were an odd couple; he so small and ineffectual; she large and powerful, rather like Russell Drysdale's painting The Drover's Wife. Very pale. Probably anaemic. Someone said she'd once been a nurse.

Charmaine Ginnane took a delicate lace handkerchief to her upturned nose. Bridie had read somewhere there were fourteen types of noses. Surreptitiously she fingered her own and wondered what type it was. Hadn't thought about her nose much, except when she had a cold when it seemed to grow twice its size and glow an incandescent red. However, there was no doubting it; Charmaine still retained the glamorous aura that had surrounded her when she was a cinema usherette.

Sam West, she knew would be focused with an eagle eye on the events, watching for any deviation from the normal. This type of thing was his speciality, and he enjoyed every moment. Beefy. Aged about forty, she thought, and she knew he was divorced but got to see his little daughter on weekends. Sad case...

Her eyes moved on to the others. Young Adele Chambers and her boyfriend Tommy Vincent sat holding hands. The casual dress brigade; he in shredded jeans and T-Shirt; she mousy with glasses and ratty hair in a ponytail. Both were absorbed in the hideous scourging. Sympathetic youngsters were always a good sign and augured well for the future. Muriel always chatted with them. She didn't have any children so maybe she enjoyed their company. Made up for what was missing in her life.

Tall languid, Lance Benson sat slightly apart from the others. Always did. A bit of a loner thought Bridie. She wondered what he did after these events. He always seemed to sidle away from the group and disappear. She knew he lived alone and had two cats, but that was the limit of her knowledge.

A quick intake of breath from the others transported Bridie from her wool-gathering, and she watched as a nail was hammered violently into the open palm of a hand. She glanced at her watch again. Must be on the move soon. They will want their tea and biscuits. As she rose to go her handbag tipped over and a set of keys clattered to the floor. She held her breath and glanced at the others. Joe stirred slightly in his sleep, but each appeared focused on the torture. Swiftly she gathered the keys and made her way out. She smiled to herself; old Max was not there - again.

Chapter Two

Belinda Lawrence stood on the corner of Flinders & Swanston streets, outside St Paul's Cathedral while waiting for the green light. Her thoughtful eyes followed the throng discharging from the rail station, sometimes veiled by the hulking, clangourous trams rattling across the intersection. Her mood was one of nostalgia blended with melancholy. The lights turned green, and along with the bustling crowd, Belinda made her way across to Federation Square. Her nostalgia stemmed from a return to her hometown of Melbourne and the gossamer memories it invoked. Melancholy from her recent breakup with her lover Mark Sallinger which, while undeniably justified, left an unexpected emptiness in her life along with a dispiriting ache lurking in the shadows.

The crossing complete, the Square lay before her, crowded now in the late summer sun with lunchtime diners, noisy college groups draped around the ochre-coloured sandstone blocks, fiddling with smartphones and taking selfies. Some tone-deaf street musicians added to the maelstrom of Melbourne at play.

Belinda turned from this and made her way along Flinders Street to the Australian Centre for the Moving Image. A large white acronym ACMI indicated she had arrived at her destination. The cinema programme had listed some films Belinda wanted to see, and she had agreed to meet up with Hazel Whitby who had gone on a shopping spree. A mixture of various film soundtracks emanating from a large display area drew Belinda into 'Screen Worlds The Story of Film, Television & Digital Culture', where historic fragments of a past culture's moving image were on display: early cinema cameras, projectors, television sets, all marshalled together now for exploration by a generation bewitched by smartphones, social media, downloads, and the frangibility of digital 21st century enlightenment.

A display of coloured glass slides took her attention. They appeared to be religious images depicting the life of Christ. She began to read the accompanying text.

"Belinda?"

The sharp enquiry made her turn to seek out the speaker. "Belinda Lawrence? Is that you? Approaching her with tentative gait and querulous expression was a small rotund figure draped in a voluminous pashmina shawl conspicuously emblazoned with lurid butterflies. The colourful accessories, glitzy hair ornaments, fingers heavy with rings, armbands and bracelets, which taken together, indicated an aficionado of fin de siècle 20th-century fashion. And crowning her head, hair the colour of straw, tipped with a purple tint, was held in the fashion of a distraught haystack, completing what the woman no doubt believed expressed her individuality and charisma.

A faint memory stirred in the back of

Belinda's brain.

"Belinda! It's me. Bridie Kelly." A wide smile creased the woman's face as she clutched at Belinda's arm.

Images of gymslips and the faint clink of hockey sticks flooded Belinda's memory; Bridie Kelly, class swat, amateur thespian (her Lady Macbeth inspired excessive deployment of hand lotion among Year Ten scholars) and all-around eccentric.

"Oh, Bridie! You haven't changed a bit," said Belinda, as she tried to extricate her arm from Bridie's grasp.

"I haven't seen you since you went off to Uni," chattered Bridie enthusiastically, "let me look at you." She stepped back to evaluate her old school chum. What she saw was an apparition of what she had once aspired to but had failed, so miserably, to accomplish: Belinda had retained her slim build and figure, dressed now in a cream linen trouser suit. Her complexion clear, with one or two small wrinkles that come naturally as one approaches thirty: bright blue eyes, honey coloured hair: all in all, an attractive woman at her peak.

"I heard you inherited a mansion in South Kensington," babbled Bridie, "after your aunt, who was a murderer and..."

Belinda was startled. "Nothing of the kind! My great aunt was murdered, and I inherited her cottage, not in South Kensington, but in Bath."

Bridie chose to be agnostic towards this

claim. A poor substitute for the grapevine scandal she had spread over many luncheon tables. "Not what I heard. Still, if you say so. But you did get involved selling antiques?"

"Yes. With Hazel. Hazel Whitby. You might meet her. We arranged to see a film here."

However, Bridie would not be distracted from her inquisition. "And aren't you engaged to a knight or a baron, or something? Anyway, someone with a title. We always said you'd make good. Will you be married here or in London?"

A shadow passed over Belinda's face as she finally broke free from Bridie's control. "Well, sadly the engagement is off."

Bridie pulled a face indicating disappointment but masking her desire to hear all the intricate details behind that explosive news. She was about to express fabricated sympathy when her attention was taken by an event she witnessed over Belinda's shoulder. Her eyes grew narrow, and her lips tightened into a disapproving line.

Belinda, startled by the woman's expression, turned to see the cause. A thin young man, dressed in black jeans, T-shirt and coat, stepped from the escalator and hurried toward the downstairs exhibition centre. He brushed long black hair from his face, a face now distorted in anger. She heard Bridie utter the critical words. "The Turk!"

***

Jake G. Schwantz rushed across the foyer and careered down the steps. His long-fingered hand once more pushed languid hair from his eyes as he brushed violently past visitors on their way to the current film exhibition. His rage now took the form of expletives spilling from his bloodless lips, as in his mind he performed excruciating torture on his obstructionists. They were all a bunch of '*has-been*' oldies! More like '*never been*'. How did he ever think they would understand what he was proposing? Couldn't they see how they could all benefit from his scheme? Was he wasting his time with them? But of course, they held the upper hand. He hated to admit it, but without them, or at least some of them, he couldn't put his plan into action. Who in the group was the most pliable? More open to suggestion? He gave a thin smile. Of course, Joe O'Brien!

***

Joe O'Brien put down a treasured if battered copy of WHEN THE LION ROARS, containing the sacred writings from Metro-Goldwyn-Mayer's publicity department circa 1943. He took a sip of tea. Girl Crazy, with Mickey and Judy. Also, little June Allyson made her first screen appearance. Joe chuckled. He'd been in love with June Allyson. Not really of course; he loved Muriel, his wife of how many years? Pity Muriel didn't share his nostalgia. She was in the kitchen making a sponge cake to take to the meeting of the group later that night. Joe looked thoughtful as the magazine slid from his lap. The group. They'd been meeting together now for, how long? His memory was getting poor. You read so much about Alzheimer's. Did he have it? He must talk to his doctor. If he remembered. Now, what had he been thinking about? – Ah yes, the group. Old Max hadn't been at the last meeting. That was odd. He rarely missed out. Odd too, that young fellow, Jake, the one they called The Turk had got involved with them. Strange boy. He recalled someone telling him something about a plan the boy had. Now, who said that? Lance? No, of course. It was Harry Winters.

***

Harry Winters stepped from the shower and briskly dried his body. He carried out this ritual as usual before the full-length mirror which afforded the sight of his seventy-year-old body. Also, as usual, he smiled in admiring approval at his reflection. He still had it. Those years of sporting activity had paid off. His smiled increased. It afforded him the luxury of more pleasant physical activity nowadays which some men half his age would find punishing. Punishing! The word amused him. He ran a critical eye over his stomach. Not a six- pack, but still firm, no beer gut there. He flexed his biceps.

Punish.

Scourge.

He'd like to scourge that young turk, Jake. Sticking his nose into others business. Still, what he was proposing had some merit. It also gave food for thought. Why did one need Jake? Why did one need the others in the group? If old Max alone had the answer, a one-on-one deal could be arranged. He pulled on his clothes. Old Max hadn't answered the phone recently; he gave an amused grunt. Well, maybe he was having some difficulties. Fully dressed now, another glance in the mirror confirmed he still had it. A dab of cologne here and there. That new little bar would be open. He might get lucky again. A thought crossed his mind. Why had he thought of her? Of Charmaine?

***

Charmaine Ginnane applying her mascara paused in mid-stroke. Harry Winters. Why had she thought of Harry Winters? Ah yes, he said he had a proposition to make. Charmaine studied her reflection. Makeup perfect. Her jawline was still strong. Crow's feet? Well, not enough to be labelled a 'Murder' she joked to herself. All in all, not bad for sixty – no, she wouldn't continue that line of thought.

Still, her figure hadn't thickened, maybe a little, but she could even get into her maroon usherette slacks that added a touch of 'Hollywood': or so the management had thought. The slacks rested now in the back of her cupboard, not so much a relic but a reminder of past glories: they accentuated her long legs. Thinking of the past returned her thoughts to Harry. To him it had always been a bit of slap and tickle; she'd always wanted something permanent. It hadn't happened of course, but she sensed Harry was about to attempt to stoke the embers once more.

She wondered if he knew of her affair with Max? Why they called him 'old Max' was silly really: he was only a year or so older than most of the group. Probably because he had been in the business longer than most. He hadn't been seen recently, but that was not unusual; everyone knew he often went off unannounced, usually up to the Gold Coast so it could be assumed that was where he was.

Charmaine slipped into her Chanel Tweed coat. She was looking forward to the screening tonight. But first...

Chapter Three

"Old Max started it. It's like a..." Bridie searched for the words, "...like a film society, I suppose that's the best way to describe it." The three women had adjourned to the ACMI café, and while Belinda and Bridie took coffee, Hazel, true to her intoxicating tradition had guzzled a gin and tonic and was already setting about her second. She needed refreshment badly, for her shopping expedition had been disastrous; nothing in her colours, practically nothing her size, only one Gucci item purchased, sales staff lacking in basic people skills and young enough to be in primary school. That irritated Hazel the most; their rudeness was bad enough, but the age gap between them and herself rankled, and she was, once again, forced to re-consider employing the maxim, 'those of more mature years should precede younger people', but found this difficult as her life-long bon mot had always been, 'beauty before the beast'.

Bridie took a break from her dissertation and sipped on her iced coffee. Hazel Whitby viewed her through critical eyes. Bovine. They probably milk her twice a day, was her uncharitable and entirely incorrect assessment of Belinda's old school chum. She recognised the harshness of that judgment, made while flushed with pique, - those surly shop girls had a lot to answer for - and had the good grace to be ashamed. This was a novelty which surprised her and gave, if not elevation to sainthood, at least a comfortable self-righteous aura of transcendence.

Hazel would be surprised if she could hear Bridie's silent assessment of herself. While not as vulgar as she'd been, Bridie's view was probably more accurate. 'Mutton!' was her brief observation; tall with a black Louise Brooks page-boy bob (circa 1929 and probably the year of her birth) while dressed in the present-day fashions Bridie abhorred. English, and probably a snob. How did Belinda ever get to be friends with her?

Belinda broke into her judgement. "What kind of film society?"

"Oh, it's a group of aged cinema projectionists or others who've worked in movie theatres in the old days. You know, screening films before digital took over and having the girl in the candy-bar push a button and the film starts."

"So they lost their jobs?"

"Pretty much so."

"But why a film society?"

"Well, it's not so much a society; most projectionists usually had copies of films on celluloid. Once a film had done all its screenings the print was usually dumped, and often the projectionist would save them, or some reels of a film, for his collection. Most have films dating way back, and it became a game to see who could collect the oldest film as well as the most popular."

"And how did you get involved with them," asked Hazel lethargically.

"Oh, I teach film studies at our old school," said Bridie, with an egotistical smile. Belinda wasn't the only one from our class that made good. "I introduce the cinematic arts to students with a range of media including documentary, feature and short films, internet content and all that. My students plan, make, and distribute their little works. That way they develop an appreciation of the art, with hands-on filmmaking skills. Somewhere along the line, we had one of these projectionists give a talk to the students; he invited me to their weekly private screenings, and I just sort of got involved and loved hearing all their stories from the bio box."

"The what box?" asked Hazel.

"The Bio Box; the room in the cinemas where the projectors were installed," said Bridie knowledgeably, "Look," she added brightly, "there's a screening at the Society tonight. Why not come with me? I'm sure I can take guests."

Belinda and Hazel exchanged looks; Hazel mouthing a silent 'NO!' Belinda giving a shrug of acceptance. After all, they had nothing planned, and it might prove to be amusing. She felt the need for a diversion to help lift her mood.

Bridie gave a whoop of joy. "Great. I'm sure you'll love it. Old Max may not be there, I think he's away, but most of the others in the group will be."

Hazel's displeasure showed signs of returning, and she muttered dangerously, "What are they screening?"

"Don't know," said Bridie. "They take it in

turns to screen a film from their collection. It's usually a secret until the title appears on the screen; it could be a silent film or maybe a musical. Who knows, but it's always fun." Belinda hid a smile at Hazel's ferocious expression. They rose to go. "I'll pick you up about seven. Where are you staying?"

"At my parent's house in East Melbourne, you'd remember it I'm sure," said Belinda. "They're away on a six-month cruise at the moment." The women exited the café into the open space of Federation Square, Bridie babbling on about old school gossip, Hazel trailing behind petulantly scheming ways to avoid the evening screening.

Seated nearby in the shadows and watching their departure with interest was The Turk - Jake G. Schwantz. As they made their way into the noisy crowd, he rose to follow them.

Chapter Four

Jake sucked the blood off his thumb. A shard of glass had sliced into his flesh as he reached in through the shattered window. Turning the old lock had been difficult but eventually yielded to his insistence. Tentatively he pushed open the door and stepped into a small porch.

His feet crunched on the broken glass scattered on the worn linoleum. To his left he could see the kitchen; ahead a passage led to the main rooms of the house. Cold and silent, the air musty with damp and dust. Max it seemed was away. Now was a perfect time. The floor boards objected to his advance, squeaking and groaning, all amplified in the hush of the empty house.

Wrapping a handkerchief around his bleeding thumb, he continued until he reached the entrance hall. He knew the rooms that ran off to the side; a dining room, a reception chamber which led to a garden room attached to the side of the building like one of Prince Charles' carbuncles. Knew them well as he'd often attended one of Max's 'soirees' as the old fool liked to call them; just a piss-up was more like it in Jake's vernacular. No. What he wanted was upstairs in one of the six or seven rooms.

Possibly.

Hopefully.

He glanced up at the stained-glass window

on the landing. The early evening sunlight beaming through scattered a rainbow of violent shapes on the walls, creating a mystical grotto turning the simple staircase into a Jacob's Ladder. Totally unaware of this biblical transformation, Jake climbed swiftly. He didn't have much time. It was probably foolish to have left it so late, but now he was here he had to do what he had planned.

The sound of a car approaching and drawing to a stop made him pause. He peered out of the landing window. In a rose-coloured world, he saw Bridie, and the two strange women he'd seen earlier in the day emerge from the car. Shit! Even less time now. He turned and began the climb to the top floor. Reaching the passage, he paused at the door on his right. Closed. The ornate brass handle, long unpolished, was ice cold, but readily capitulated to his firm grip. Silently the door swung open revealing...

***

"It's Old Max's wife, Sheila's family home," said Bridie. Belinda closed the car door and looked up at the large double-storied Victorian house. A balcony on the upper floor ran the width of the building. Below, floor to ceiling windows looked out over a park. Beyond, the city skyline, now beginning to twinkle in the darkening sky, was ominously close, so she knew they were in one of the inner- city northern suburbs, suburbs that held memories of Melbourne's early history. Farmland, then residences of politicians and the upwardly mobile, then sinking back to become homes for the workers in nearby factories built for the burgeoning city, to be liberated and fashionable once more, while all the late Victorian structures retained their elegance and defied capricious fashions.

"Seems Sheila's great-grandfather struck it lucky in the gold rush," continued Bridie, as she led Belinda and Hazel down the wide side driveway, "he built this on the proceeds and the family have been here ever since."

"Are they still here?" asked Hazel.

"Only Max. His inherited it when his wife died. Two brothers are dead, and his only sister lives somewhere in Pennsylvania. In a nursing home. Ga-Ga apparently."

They were approaching a red brick building separate from the house. Bridie paused to rest. She was beginning to find walking and talking at the same time challenging and wondered if it was the beginning of a slide into old age, eventually to find herself in a state of Ga-Ga-ness. "This was a caretaker's house," she puffed, "and stables. Max had it converted into his private cinema, and this is where we screen our films." She glanced at her watch. "The others should be here already. Let's join them."

***

Jake slid the heavy drapes aside allowing muted light to assault the dark bedroom. The four-poster bed with the rumpled sheets and blankets was of no interest to him. A dresser took his attention. Each drawer he pulled out, the contents he flung aside. Occasionally he paused when some papers were revealed. He scanned them quickly; no, not what he wanted. The documents joined the shirts and underwear on the carpet. He stood erect. Disappointed. A glance around the room revealed a sizeable ornate wardrobe. Jake swung the doors open. Nothing there either, apart from a few dispirited suits awaiting resuscitation by human inhabitancy. Pulling a chair across he climbed on it and felt around the top of the wardrobe. Dust. Nothing else. A sigh of disappointment. Still, there were the other rooms. He stepped out into the passage and moved to the next door.

***

"This is Belinda and her English friend, Hazel," Bridie said, introducing them to the group. The atmosphere was uneasy, and questioning glances were exchanged among the group. Belinda wondered why.

Harry drew himself up, tightened his stomach muscles and winked at Belinda.

Charmaine ran a critical eye over Hazel. Hazel returned the assessment. An unspoken enmity now existed.

Joe smiled vacantly. He hadn't caught their names.

Muriel flinched slightly at the knowledge Hazel was 'English'.

Adele and Tommy smiled like two puppies and murmured ineffectual greetings.

Sam gave a half-smile and shuffled his feet.

Lance gave a faint nod of acceptance and stared at the floor.

A silence ensued, broken by Bridie, "I'm sure you'll welcome them both to the screening tonight. What is it to be?" She glanced anxiously around the indifferent faces. Had she breached an accepted covenant by bringing guests unannounced?

Lance gave a slight cough. "It's my choice tonight. Some reels from Sweet Rosie O'Grady".

Bridie gave a sigh of relief. "Oh good, a musical. Betty Grable, am I right? Something light. 1943? 1945?" She turned to Belinda and Hazel. "Last week we had Sam's film, 'From the Manger to the Cross'. A silent film, 1912, but very bloodthirsty. A bit boring really. The predictable end was certainly an anti-climax."

Hazel whispered to Belinda, "What is she? The antipodean Leonard Maltin?" Belinda bit back a grin.

Bridie glanced around in case Sam had heard her derogatory remark, but he seemed not to have. Belinda looked to the group. "Thank you all for allowing us to join you tonight. We're very privileged." She gave an engaging smile, and the group responded, not so ardently, but at least the ice was broken. Except for Hazel and Charmaine who, each identifying an enemy within the castle ramparts, bridled elegantly. Belinda grinned as the two icebergs moved as far away from each other as was possible in the small and crowded space.

The tiny theatre was fitted out with some of the more comfortable seats from a long-gone cinema and on one wall a screen with non-functional side curtains. Opposite, the small windows of the projection room revealed a glimpse of an old projector. Off to the side, a small kitchen promised chilled drinks and Muriel's sponge cake.

While Lance disappeared into the projection room, each took a seat and settled back to gaze in wonder at Betty Grable's million-dollar legs.

"I remember this film," said Charmaine, who privately thought she'd match her legs against Betty's anytime, "one critic said, 'Pretty as a bowl of wax fruit and just as dull'."

"Shush," admonished Muriel, as she settled her large frame comfortably. She liked a good musical.

The lights dimmed, and a beam of light flooded the screen. Violent 20th Century Fox Technicolor dazzled their eyes and Grable was revealed prancing across the screen in Hollywood's idea of 19th-century burlesque. Full-length gloves; a be-feathered hat; a giant bow on her derriere, all designed to frame the most famous legs in show business. The brash over-orchestrated music deafened them, so they hardly heard the door open.

It wasn't until Jake staggered in front of the screen, the diffused Technicolor streaming across his body, his raised hand attempting to block out the projector light, that the audience became aware of him.

It also became aware of the blood flowing from his hand and down his body.

"Max!" shouted Jake, above Betty's warbling, "Max is dead! Murdered!"

Chapter Five

Max's body lay on the floor, his shirt open revealing matted grey hairs. His bound hands grasped in an attitude of prayer. There wasn't much left of his head.

The group gathered at the door, each face showing shock as they took in the horror before them. Charmaine gave a loud scream, covered her face and began to wail. Muriel, who seemed remarkably calm, placed an arm around her shoulder and drew her back into the passage. Sam started to retch and, covering his mouth, stumbled back down the stairs. Adele buried her face in Tommy's T-shirt his arms encircling her.

Belinda and Hazel edged their way to the front of the group. There was a stunned silence as each tried to adjust to the reality before them.

Jake was shivering with shock. "That's how I found him. I was just..." his voice trailed off. Yes, thought Belinda, what were you doing?

Muriel, a tower of strength in an emergency, bustled back and took Jake by the arm. "Come with me, dear. I'm making some strong sweet tea for Charmaine. You're both in shock." She guided him and Charmaine along the passage and downstairs.

The others exchanged worried glances. "What should we do?" whimpered Bridie.

Harry Winters edged closer to the corpse and bent to cover the old man's naked chest and untie the ropes around his legs.

"I wouldn't do that," said Belinda, sharply.

Harry turned to her. "What? Who are you to give orders?"

"Nothing should be touched until the police arrive."

"I don't need you to tell me what to do. We can't let him be found like this."

"Why not?" said Hazel. "D'you think he cares about his appearance now?"

Harry glared at the two women. He wasn't used to being told what to do by females.

Lance gave a slight cough. "They are right, Harry. Let him be and call the police." Harry grunted, stood up and stormed out of the room.

Tommy let go of Adele and fumbled in his jacket pocket. "I'll phone them." He produced a phone and punched in 000.

"I think we should all leave. Is there a lock on the door?" said Belinda.

The remaining group edged into the passage. "Yes," said Adele. There's a big old key." Belinda began to herd the others out of the room. She whispered to Hazel, "Have a quick look around and see if you can find any clues."

In the hallway Tommy was talking on the phone, giving the police the details and address. He switched off the call. "The cops will be here in a few minutes. They said to leave everything as it is."

As the group began to descend the staircase, Hazel joined Belinda at the door. "Some things of interest. I'll tell you later."

Belinda closed the door and locked it. Removing the key and holding it tightly, she and Hazel followed the others to await the arrival of the police. The group was silent but kept a distance from each other as though they could be contaminated by close contact.

Tommy was further away from them and talking quietly but furiously into his phone. Adele stood near him listening to his hushed conversation and watching the others as one would privately appraise the value in a herd of sheep, until she was gathered up to be comforted by Muriel and spirited away to be given her magic bullet, calming sweet tea.

***

"Did you notice the bruises on his body?" said Hazel, as she added a dollop of sour cream to her bowl of deep ruby Borsch. It was the night after the discovery of Max's body and the first opportunity the two women had to discuss the events. The group had all been interviewed and fingerprinted. As all members, including Belinda and Hazel, were under suspicion the police acted on new laws which allowed them to obtain DNA samples without waiting for Court approval. They then advised that no one was to leave the city while awaiting the result of the DNA and an autopsy.

"Meaning he'd been beaten before the blow

that killed him?" said Belinda, topping up their glasses with a vigorous, crimson Shiraz.

"Yes. So?"

"Bashed him first in a rage? And then killed him."

"But why?"

Belinda shrugged. "Who knows? Because he wouldn't co-operate with the murderer? Did you find anything in the room that provided a clue?"

"Not really. It seems to be a sort of storeroom. Lots of film equipment, cameras, and projectors that sort of thing. Rows of cans that I suppose held films. One odd thing. There were some religious pictures. They seemed out of place." Hazel was silent for a moment and toyed with her soup spoon, making circles in the Borsch. "Bashed him and then killed him?" she mused. "Assuming it was one person did both." Hazel glanced at Belinda. "You think there was more than one?"

Belinda pushed her soup bowl away. Suddenly she didn't feel hungry. "It's possible. After all, the group..."

"You mean someone in the group is guilty?"

"Well, it was hardly a robbery gone wrong. And the police certainly don't think so. He was tied up and gagged and apparently had been like that for some time. It seems odd no one in the group had seen him for some time, just assuming he was on holiday."

"Or so they say."

Belinda nodded. "Right. One of them could

be lying."

"Or all of them?"

"If so, why?"

"Unless there's something about Max's private life that they and we don't know?"

Belinda yawned. "Hazel. Life isn't always like some of the books you read. What was it, Fifty Shades of Grey Flannel?"

Hazel gave a deprecating smile. "There are stranger things on earth, you know. But seriously, was he involved with someone in the group? Was there conflict between them?"

Belinda took a sip of wine. "It's possible. However, I think there's something else."

Hazel became reflective. "I'd like to have a good look around the house. Young Jake, he broke in. Why, and what was he looking for?"

"Checking on Max?" said Belinda. "Was going to find out what was behind Max's apparent disappearance?"

Hazel frowned. "Could be. So, he broke in, discovered Max was home. They had an argument, the kid lost his temper and bashed in his head."

"While he was trussed up like a Christmas turkey?" Belinda was silent for a moment. "No. No, I don't think it was Jake who killed Max. Think about how he burst into the screening. He was scared witless. That's why he's been hospitalised with shock and under police guard until he can be questioned again. Anyway, police will check on the blood samples. As the one who discovered the body and had Max's blood mingled with his own on his wounded hand, he was their chief suspect."

"Talking of blood. There has to be blood on the clothes of the attacker."

"And what was, and where is, the murder weapon?"

"Whatever's behind all this has to be in the house, I'm sure of it," said Hazel, draining her glass. "What say we take a look?"

Belinda stifled another yawn. The excitement of the past days was catching up with her, and the proposition of sinking into her welcoming soft bed was becoming imperative. "I wish you luck. The police forensic boffins have sealed the house and no doubt spent time gathering as much information as they could, given the cluttered state of the place." Her eyelids drooped. "While we waited for the police, I managed to get a look at some rooms. They were topsy-turvy...with a chaotic...hotchpotch of... one strange thing ... photos...they looked familiar... but I can't..." Belinda's head fell forward, chin onto her breast. Sound asleep.

Hazel frowned at her. Had her friend really got over her breakup with Mark Sallinger? They had been together for a number of years and came close to marrying until Belinda finally realised it was a wrong choice. Hazel herself had never liked him. Handsome, yes. Wealthy, yes. A baronet if you please, but...he reminded her of her ex-husband whose only love was money. Lust, of course, was another matter and he had given in to those enchantments outside of marriage. She felt Mark was cut from the same cloth.

Belinda gave a faint snore.

Really, the young ones these days had no stamina. In my day... Hazel reached for the wine bottle.

***

Charmaine stared at her face in the mirror. Twenty-four hours of weeping plus tortuous questioning at the police station had taken its toll. She looked like a circus clown. What make-up remained was streaked and patchy. Wearily she pulled her hair back and saturated a cotton pad with eye makeup remover.

Would she ever rid her mind of the image of Max's wounded head? Tears trickled down her cheek. She brushed them aside and held the cotton pad against her closed eye. Best not to think of that. Best to...best to what? Max had proposed marriage. She'd thought about it. An affair is one thing. Marriage another. But Max had money, she knew that, and it would make her future that much more comfortable. She liked Max. A lot.

She began to remove the remnants of mascara that had eluded her tears. She didn't love Max; was 'liking a lot' enough reason to marry? That was a stupid question now; Max was dead. What little lipstick lingering on her lips was smudged. She spread a film of petroleum jelly on them. She had to think.

Who guessed it would end this way? And would it have been worth it? A small amount of coconut oil in the palms of her hands and she began to rub it onto her face.

It had seemed, at first, a good idea, and was assumed Max would go along with it. After all, there'd be some benefit to it. Who'd have thought his reaction would be so violent? She wondered what the others were thinking.

**

Muriel O'Brien sat listening to the rain pattering on the tin roof. The closed-in porch at the rear of the bungalow was her territory and her favourite spot in the suburban house that had been home to her and Joe since their wedding day. How many years ago? She should remember easily but always had to stop and think. She could hear Joe snoring. He slept now in the spare room; that way he didn't disturb her with his rumblings. Well, not as bad as when they shared the double bed in the front room.

Her chubby fingers finished sewing a rip in a freshly laundered cleaners' smock. That done she played idly with a crochet hook, colourful yarn nearby awaiting transformation into something from Muriel's imagination. But her attention was not on the hook or the yarn.

Staring out into the blackness of the night she conjured up Max's face. Beyond recognition. She'd been used to seeing dead bodies. But not a violently murdered person, at least in situ.

She never really understood Joe's passion for films, but over the years she had accepted it; all those years when he was working nights screening big Hollywood extravaganzas while she stayed home keeping his supper warm. Now, she could see the group gave him some comfort in his retirement. A strange lot of people. Not her sort at all, but again if it made Joe happy.

Also, of course, there was the other business. She had to admit it was all a bit of a mystery to her but could see how they would benefit from it. She glanced around at the shabby, cluttered room, and shivered, folding her arms across an ample bosom. House needed work. Repair. Would that happen now? Whom could she ask? Lance? Yes, Lance seemed more approachable than the others. Quieter. Sensible. She would talk to Lance.

***

Lance Benson sat somberly in the low light, the whirring of the old VHS cassette machine the only sound in the hushed night. Alfred Newman's melodic boisterousness had been turned off, to leave a colourless Charles Laughton's Quasimodo at a loss for words. Two cats sat, legs folded under to resemble furry tea cosies, sat, eyes fixed on their liegeman. Something was wrong. He was worried, they could tell that.

Lance *was* worried. The TV screen may as

well have been dark; he paid it no attention. Max's murder played on the screen in his mind. The hours with the police had been distressing, more so having come so soon after the shock of finding Max's body.

And why Max? Could it have been...?

Lance shook his head. No. He didn't want to think that; think it had been a result of the plan. He had finally agreed to it after the urging from the others overcame his initial reluctance. It had been discussed at great length and seemed a reasonable thing to do. After all, Max would probably see reason and approve. Any suggestion of violence had never been discussed, and if it had, he would certainly not have supported the idea. But needs must when the devil drives. He'd learnt that lesson.

He needed to talk it over with someone. Probably best to have a chat with Harry. After all, he was the one who...

***

Harry drained the last of his beer and pushed away from the bar. It was that time of night when the grating music increased in volume as the 'suits' arrived with their current office squeeze, all fresh from a company credit card meal, ready for a refreshing ale before moving on to a club and the party drug of their choice.

Out in the wet streets, he manoeuvred his way around groups of tourists keen to lap up all the excitement the city had to offer. Away from the crowds, his footsteps echoed in the night. Occasionally splashing in puddles. Max's murder came as no surprise. Not to him at least. He wondered how the others in the group were handling it. They hadn't had a chance to get together away from the police, but he knew that sooner or later he would be hearing from them.

The two strange women who were at the screening and later, when they discovered Max's body? Who were they? They came with Bridie. He would have to question her. What had she told them? Did they know about the plan? If so, they could cause trouble. He walked a little faster. If only he could get to talk to Jake. But the cops had him firmly under their thumb. At least for the moment. He hoped the silly little bugger hadn't given the game away. As soon as the boy was out of the hospital, he would have to...

The memory of that girl, Belinda? Taking control as she did when he tried to remove the rope from Max's body. He didn't like that. Being told what to do by a young...

Yes. She could definitely be trouble. But he could deal with that.

All it needed was a...

***

Belinda opened her eyes and blinked. It was morning. She stretched, yawned, and lay back on the pillow. She vaguely recalled falling asleep at the kitchen table, being nudged awake by Hazel and escorted upstairs to her bed. She'd slept deeply but in the minutes before waking she had a dream; a dream of a cluttered room with several doors leading to other rooms. She hadn't opened the doors but somehow knew what was behind them. More cluttered rooms; furniture piled high, broken china scattered around, religious images and, central to it all, an intangible object that remained hidden from view. All the time she sensed someone was with her, but she could never see who it was. She wondered if it was Mark, her ex-fiancé but rejected that thought. Mark was 'then' and this was 'now. She was intent on building a new life and seeking fruitful dreams. So, the accompanying presence remained a shadowy figure always on the periphery of her vision.

Her thoughts returned to the murder. And the group. She wondered if the police had made any progress toward solving the case. Presumably, they would all be interviewed by them again. Her only real source of information regarding the members of the group was Bridie.

Coffee? Or lunch?

Or a visit to her old school and catch Bridie in her 'cinematic arts' lair.

***

Bridie's burrow in the old bluestone building was divided; one section had all her students' files diligently stored, the other, Bridie's tributary, a battle zone of film paraphilia at war with digital contrivances. DVD's, film spools, books, photographs, cameras, all seeking domination in the crowded space.

Bridie wheezed as she placed yet another pile of books on what little space she could find on her desk. "I'm still in shock. To think someone would murder Max. To make it worse, it seems he was killed only three or four hours before he was found. With a blunt instrument, the police say. But why?"

"That's the question everyone is asking," said Belinda as she glanced at the books. "And also, why he was tied up and been kept a prisoner."

Bridie turned wide eyes on Belinda. "I know! How ghastly. It doesn't bear thinking about."

"Nonetheless, the police are thinking about it, and want answers."

Bridie nodded mutely.

"And it seems pretty certain they suspect a member of your group," continued Belinda, "any thoughts on that?"

"I really couldn't say," said Bridie, as she avoided Belinda's eye and studiously began to sort through the books. "As I told you the other day, I only met them recently and don't know much about anyone in particular. I only go for the films and don't socialise with them. I'm beginning to wish I hadn't met them. I mean, if I'd known one of them was a murderer, well..."

"But you must have formed an opinion about

some of them. Is there anyone in particular you think was capable of murder?"

Bridie stopped fiddling with the books and looked thoughtful. "Well, I didn't take much to Harry Winters. He made my flesh creep sometimes. Looked at me funny. Gave me the shivers."

"Looked at you how?"

"Well," said Bridie, giving a half-hearted imitation of an offended virgin, "you know, like he wanted to, you know..."

"No, I don't," said Belinda, who was not going to let her off the hook.

Bridie wiggled her shoulders, "Like he wanted to, well, make love to me."

Belinda bit back a smile. "So you think that makes him a potential murderer? Is there anyone else you suspect?"

Again Bridie looked thoughtful. "Maybe Charmaine. I think she and Harry had something going between them."

"Such as?"

Bridie glanced at her watch. "Oh, I'm running late. I've got a class due now. You'll have to excuse me." She began to gather some files and in doing so dislodged a pile of books. Belinda bent to pick them up. One caught her attention, and she stopped to inspect it.

AUSTRALIAN KINEMA
An Anthology.
By Lady Davina Stratton.

"An old book, 1920, I think. About our early films," said Bridie, "not worth bothering about." But she looked concerned as Belinda flicked through the pages. There were some illustrations of films from the beginning of the 20th Century. A page, containing sepia religious illustrations, readily fell open as though from constant use. Belinda realised she'd seen them before; the coloured slides at the ACMI exhibition.

Before she had a chance to comment on the images, Bridie snatched the book from her. "I best be off. Good to catch up again, Belinda. Can you see yourself out?' With that, she bustled away quickly to the corridor and vanished into a classroom.

Slowly Belinda made her way out of the college. She sat in the shade of a tree to wait for Hazel to arrive in her parent's car which they had the use of. In her mind, she ran over her conversation with Bridie. She was not convinced her ex-school chum was telling all she knew. And those religious pictures. She'd seen them at ACMI, realised she had seen them at Max's house, and now they were in that old book. Coincidence? And if so... She glanced at her watch, gave an exasperated sigh, and took her phone from her bag. Hazel was late.

***

Hazel was also sitting in the shade of a tree on the opposite side of the city. In the park fronting

Max's house. The Crime Scene tape was still draped around the perimeter, but there was no sign of any activity. Just why she had driven there after dropping Belinda off at the college Hazel wasn't sure. She had planned to do some more shopping in the boutiques. But some capricious instinct suggested she should swing by the murder house; an instinct that was proving to be misleading as minutes passed, and Hazel felt she was losing valuable time when she could be getting her own back on the upstart sales girl who had ruffled her feathers a few days ago (but not before she'd acquired her Gucci floral pyjama trousers. She ran an appreciative hand over the exotic fabric now covering her thigh).

The warm breeze lulled her into a soporific state, while the early autumn leaves caught up in the wind, pirouetted across the park, stopping once in a while to whirl upwards in a willy-willy. Autumn. That meant Spring back home in Bath. She and Belinda should really be going home and attending to their antique business. Her brother, Paul was managing the tiny shop on Pulteny Bridge, but in winter it was only open at the weekend for a few hours, and the larger shop in Wells was closed temporarily. Spring meant tourists and the challenge of taking their money had enormous appeal. People on holiday will buy anything, and she was a good salesman. Saleswoman? Sales Person probably, she thought sourly. Her PC credentials were happily defective. Her phone rang, and she saw it was Belinda calling. She was about to answer when a small grey car drove slowly along the street, paused for a moment outside the house and began to move off again. Hazel's keen eyes recognised the driver.

It was Harry Winters.

The phone forgotten, she leapt from the shade and into her car. Swiftly she swung it around to follow the motor as it disappeared into another street. This took her through some side streets in an area of the city that had served for many years as an industrial hub, but now was gentrified, with honest hardworking warehouses converted to frivolous apartments for young professionals, who would never deign to soil their hands with manual tasks, unlike former employees in these past temples of craftsmanship.

Harry's car pulled to a stop outside one of these apartments.

Hazel slowed and parked some distance behind. A few minutes passed before the door of the building opened, and a woman emerged. It was Charmaine. Hazel watched in surprise and amusement as she tottered to the car, five-inch heel sandals (with a glitter garnish) clattering on the footpath. When she had been safely entrenched within, the grey car moved off towards a freeway, with Hazel following at a discreet distance.

Once on the freeway, it was difficult to keep an eye on Harry; he drove erratically and changed lanes many times, but eventually he got into the left lane and onto an exit ramp. Hazel followed suit and found herself facing a large hospital. Harry parked in the only space available, and both he and Charmaine got out and entered through the central admissions entrance. With nowhere to park Hazel was forced to continue and circle the building by side streets until she was back at the entrance. Curiosity was killing Hazel; why the hospital? Was Charmaine ill? Were they visiting a patient? If so, who? A member of the group? As she approached, she was startled to see Harry and Charmaine were accompanied by a slight figure dressed in black. It was Jake – the Turk.

Hazel was forced to drive past them and stopped a little ahead. She was taking a chance they hadn't been aware they were being followed. In the rear vision mirror, she saw them bundle Jake into their car. They joined him and set off, passing Hazel on the way. Again she followed at a distance. Back via the freeway to an inner suburb lined with street cafes and fashion boutiques. In a small quiet side street, Harry brought the car to a halt, and all three hurried into a neglected, two storied Art Deco apartment block which had a large garden area with well-established trees and shrubs. Hazel continued on a little, parked further up the street, and made her way on foot back to the apartments.

A weather-worn billboard announced the property had been sold for development, if one could read it under the graffiti, and a generic illustration of an unlovable apartment tower guaranteed a purchaser a life in hell. A dilapidated row of garages behind the building painted a picture of the building's imminent downfall.

Why Harry and Charmaine had picked Jake up from the hospital and brought him here was the question uppermost in Hazel's mind. Good Samaritans? She didn't think either one fitted comfortably into that category. The fact that Jake was the police's number one suspect put a different slant on things. If he was the murderer or knew something about the murder, they possibly wanted information from him. After all, they themselves were suspects.

The problem now was, into which apartment had they taken Jake? If it was upstairs that would be difficult. A grey-haired woman emerged and made her way through the garden to the street. Hazel approached her.

"Excuse me. Can you tell me which apartment Jake lives in?" The vinegary woman stopped short, looked Hazel up and down, and brushed past her, lips frosted with solid bad-will.

Affronted, Hazel realised she would have to rely on her initiative and proceeded into the garden. Overgrown bushes made progress difficult, and it was with luck that she avoided stepping into a large fish pond, void of fish now but gleaming with lots of green algae and slimy water. Skirting this brought her closer to the building.

She could hear raised voices and recognised Charmian's shrill tones. They seemed to come from a ground floor room. Edging along the building to a side window, Hazel parted some foliage and tentatively peered in. Ragged, dirty net curtains impeded her view, but through some chinks, she could see Harry grasping Jake by the collar and shaking him. Charmaine was screaming obscenities into his ear. Jake looked pale and frightened. What Harry was saying was difficult to hear, but one remark was clear, "The negative! Where is it?" With that, Harry slapped Jake across the face. Hard.

A movement in the bushes beside Hazel, accompanied by a low growl, froze Hazel's blood and she turned to be confronted by a display of teeth that belonged to a large German Shepherd, of the canine variety. Her immediate view was the teeth were not displayed in a friendly smile and working on the theory it was wiser to lose the battle but not the war, flight suddenly seemed the cat's pyjamas.

Plunging into the bushes, she ran towards the street. The large animal considered this an invitation to follow. Which it did. Breathless and fearing carnivore damage to her recently acquired Gucci floral trousers, Hazel pushed on through the foliage. But she had forgotten one thing.

The fish pond.

Too late, and with a sensation of somersaulting in slow motion, she tripped on the edge of the pond and fell full length into the slime. A shriek, and sitting upright, green algae clinging to her, she was confronted by the dog. In close-up. It proceeded to lick her face.

Chapter Six

"You look like the creature from the green lagoon." Belinda's arch observation as she surveyed Hazel standing in the doorway, was tinged with annoyance. Her suspicion that Hazel had been engaged in a casual liaison which took preference over answering her phone call and leaving herself without transport, had been festering all afternoon. "Don't tell me. Let me guess. He said he was a lifesaver, and you replied 'I need saving' so he resuscitated you several times. Am I right?"

Hazel, white with rage under a green glaze, glared at Belinda as she sat at the computer. Through lips of string she muttered, "I'll deal with you later." A shower and burning her Gucci pyjamas were uppermost in her mind as she climbed the stairs, but bubbling beneath the surface, turbulent responses to Belinda's accusation of frivolity. Full of self-admiration, she had been tracking down a potential killer while Little Miss Goody-Goody had been lolling around on the computer probably making asinine replies to Facebook tragics.

However, Belinda's time had been better spent and through diligent research online had located on an obscure film freak's site, an eBook of Lady Davina Stratton's dissertation, and furthermore, copies of the religious photographs that had intrigued her. So when Hazel eventually arrived fresh from her ablutions and already halfway through a G&T, she found Belinda's chagrin had dissipated, and she was bubbling over with excitement. "I think I'm onto something. You remember the religious pictures you saw in Max's house? Do you recognise them?"

Hazel peered at the images on the computer screen. "Hard to tell. I only had a quick glimpse of them, but they look similar."

"They come from an old film."

Hazel was not impressed. She felt her news to be eminently more important, not to mention exciting. She was about to make this thought common knowledge, but...

"Actually from an old Australian film," continued Belinda, "or rather something that is considered to be the first feature film ever made."

"Right," said Hazel, determined to impress with her knowledge of Jake, Harry, and Charmaine, "let me tell you what I've –"

"The Salvation Army made it in nineteen hundred," continued Belinda, her eyes glued to the computer screen, "it's probably not the world's first feature film. Auguste and Louis Lumière made 'The life and the passion of Jesus Christ'earlier, but it was only a short, about ten or eleven minutes. And there were other short films but –"

"The Salvation Army?" interrupted Hazel with some asperity. She felt the issue was heading into the realms of whimsy, not to mention a theological combat zone.

Oblivious to Hazel's sneering tone, Belinda

continued, "Yes. Made here in Melbourne by the Salvation Army. Their Limelight Department. Called 'Soldiers of the Cross', it was really an illustrated lecture. Apparently, they often gave such lectures to groups. In this case, they mixed coloured glass slides with brief film segments, filmed with actors playing the parts of Christ and Christian martyrs. Film was so new then it must have had a big effect on audiences to see biblical scenes come to life. Based on all this, some argue it is the first dramatic narrative film screened."

Interested in spite of her derision Hazel asked, "Why are you so excited by this?"

Belinda looked up from the screen. "The presentation took a bit over two hours. It was made up of two hundred glass slides, some of which have survived. Copies of them are at ACMI, where I first saw them. Then again today I saw them in a book. More importantly, we both saw copies of the photos in Max's house. It seems there were fifteen film segments of ninety seconds each."

Hazel groaned. "Fascinating history, I'm sure, but I don't see why you're so excited."

Belinda turned back to the screen again and highlighted a sentence. "Because no film segments from Soldiers of the Cross have survived and are considered to be lost cultural heirlooms. Priceless."

Hazel grunted and sank down onto a nearby sofa. "OK. So they're priceless. But I still don't see the connection with the group and Max's murder. Besides I've got some real news.'

Belinda turned to look at her. "What?"

"I know where Jake lives. I've seen him."

"But he's in hospital."

Hazel finished her drink and gave a shake of her head. "No. No. He's been released, or so it seems."

"But the police put him there under guard."

"Well they have let him out, no doubt under strict orders to report to them regularly. He may be the chief suspect, but it looks like they have nothing definite that they can charge him with. Yet. So no doubt they will be keeping an eye on him. Meanwhile, I suppose they will continue checking up on all the members."

"Do you think they believe we'd only met the group that night and had no reason to murder Max?"

Hazel shrugged, inspecting the bottom of her empty glass. "I suspect the others are more likely to be under suspicion." She rose and peered at the computer screen. "So what makes you think this old film has anything to do with the group. And the murder?"

"Just a hunch. The coincidence of the photos being in Max's house."

"Pretty thin coincidence. If he was a film freak, there is every chance he would have known about the missing film, but nothing to say that he –" She stood erect. "Unless…"

"Unless what?"

Hazel sat down again and leant close to

Belinda. "I said I knew where Jake lives. What I didn't tell you is I followed Harry and Charmaine who collected him from the hospital."

"So? They were being friendly."

"Hmm. Friendly as in 'who needs enemies when you have friends like that'. From what I saw there was no love lost." She related the events of the afternoon and watching Harry and Charmaine threaten Jake. "Charmaine was shrieking like Barbara Stanwyck on steroids, and Harry giving Clint Eastwood a run for his money. Still, I managed to hear some of the threats and heard Harry say, 'Where is it?'"

Belinda frowned. "Where's what?"

Hazel settled back into the cushions, a look of 'cat got the cream' on her face. "You know, I think you're onto something with this missing heritage film."

"Why suddenly do you think there's a connection?"

Hazel, licking fictive cream from her lips, whispered dramatically, "Because, while Harry was pummelling the kid, he shouted, 'The negative? Where is it?'"

***

Late afternoon light presented the garden of Jake's apartment building as a secretive grove but fortunately there was enough light to reveal the pathway. Following its uneven track, Belinda and

Hazel reached the front door.

"There's no security," said Belinda, "not a good sign."

"Owners too lousy to be bothered," said Hazel, as she pushed open the door, "Probably cheap rental until they can develop the site."

They stepped into the hall, and various odours assaulted their senses. Onions frying. Marijuana. Cat's pee. Enduring damp. Also, something their nasal dexterity could not define. If indeed it could be defined.

Hazel reached into her tote bag and produced a spray container of Chanel Coco Eau de Parfum, with which she saturated Belinda and herself.

"Which is Jake's apartment?" coughed Belinda, fanning the spray away.

"This one on the left," said Hazel, "I think he's home, if that ghastly rock music is any indication." She gave a rousing thump on the door. Instantly the music stopped, and all was quiet within. Hazel knocked again. Loudly. There was no reaction. Except, behind them, the squeak of a door opening and an increase in frying onion pungency.

Peering at them, from the sanctity of her burrow, the querulous woman Hazel had encountered on her previous visit. Twining around her swollen ankles, an equally disgruntled cat. That accounts for the Pee, thought Hazel, and she began to identify the undefinable odour with the woman. The cat, indicating its intention to venture into the hall, spied Hazel, hesitated, eyes widening, before fleeing for safety behind the fortification of its owner. Its owner did much the same.

Hazel's glare had sent a shiver down the woman's spine, and she quickly retreated. The door shut and there was the sound of numerous locks being activated. That diversion over, Hazel once again battered on Jake's door.

There was shuffling sounds and a muffled enquiry. "Who is it?"

"We're friends of Bridie. Belinda and Hazel. We were with the group the night Max was murdered. We'd like to talk to you," said Belinda in a voice she hoped conveyed sympathy.

There was a short silence, a click, and the door opened to reveal a security chain in place. Peering over the chain, a pale-faced Jake sized up his visitors. "I don't know you."

"But we know you," said Hazel, "and we know what Harry and Charmaine did to you."

Jake gave a start. He looked from one woman to the other. After a pause, he released the chain and opened the door. Belinda and Hazel followed him into the apartment. Belinda was reminded of her student days when walls were covered with posters of Paul Newman and Marylyn, side by side with radical political ringleaders each plying his or her guaranteed universal salve. Jake's room, in contrast, was papered with film posters from every generation from Edwin S. Porter on. A Panthéon to cinematic art; sublime and spurious. Jake flung himself onto a worn and grubby sofa from where he evaluated his visitors. "What's this about Harry and Charmaine?"

"Let's not beat about the bush," said Hazel. "We know they roughed you up over a missing negative."

"What negative?" said Jake.

"That's for you to know and for you to tell us," said Belinda.

"Don't know what you're talking about," muttered Jake.

"I think you do," said Belinda, "and I think it has something to do with 'Soldiers of the Cross'." Jake was instantly alert. He glanced from Belinda to Hazel.

"Let's go back to the night of Max's murder," said Hazel. She was about to sit in an armchair, but the stains on the upholstery looked malignant. And fresh. She tipped a collection of Sight & Sound magazines off a kitchen chair and sat leaning towards Jake. "Now, I don't believe you killed Max, but I do think you know more than you're letting on. Firstly, I'd like to know what you were doing in his house on the night of the murder, and why he was being kept prisoner there?"

"I didn't know he was a prisoner."

"Well, if it wasn't you who kept him tied up, who was it?

Jake shrugged. "Search me. Could have been anyone."

"Of the group?"

Jake nodded.

"Anyone in particular?"

"Ask *them*. I don't know. I thought he'd just gone away on a holiday. He was like that. He'd just take off and then turn up a few days later."

"So you thought you'd take advantage of him being away to break into his house and have a search. For what?"

Jake's feathers were ruffled. "I don't have to tell you anything. I've already told the cops all I know. Just who are you anyway?"

"A couple of old broads who are trying to help you," said Hazel.

Belinda, making a note to clobber Hazel for suggesting she was an 'old broad', decided to play the good cop. "Jake," she said softly, "we know it has something to do with the missing film, 'Soldiers of the Cross'. Bridie, who introduced us to the group, is an old friend of mine." (She chose to overlook the fact they hadn't seen each other in decades.) "And I just want to help her," she continued, "particularly if she is going to be accused of murder."

Jake looked at her unbelievingly. "You can't think that lump of lard could kill anyone?"

"I don't think her weight problem need be an issue here," said Belinda with some asperity, "the point is, Max was killed, and there has to be a reason. We are certain it has to do with the missing film. Did he have it?"

Jake looked at her for a moment and gave a sly grin. "He may have. And again he may not have."

"What's that supposed to mean?" snapped

Hazel.

Jake rose and stretched in an exaggerated manner. "Whatever you want it to mean. Now, get out. I've had enough of this. I didn't kill Max, and that's all I'm going to say." He opened the door and gestured to the hall. Belinda and Hazel exchanged a glance and began to leave. As she brushed past Jake, Hazel gave him a searching look. The look was returned with an arrogant smile.

Stepping out into the garden they were surprised by the almost total darkness. No light was visible to guide them on their way. Holding their hands before them and brushing past bushes they set out in the direction of the street.

"I'd like to wring his neck. There's a lot more he can tell us," said Hazel, her pace increasing as her anger grew. "But clearly he doesn't want to." Blindly she thrust her way through the heavy foliage. "That leaves the other members of the group. I'm beginning to think they're all guilty. If I had my way, I'd -"

Belinda gasped. "Look out!"

Too late. A glutinous splash and an agonising yelp indicated that once again, Hazel had fallen into the fish pond.

***

Harry parked his car in the ill-lit street. An extraordinary sight made him pause as he was about to open the door. From the dense foliage in the garden opposite a glistening slimy figure emerged. A woman followed. A woman who seemed to be holding back laughter, not too successfully. As they approached a nearby car, he saw who they were. "Our two troublemakers."

With much ado, the women managed to get into their car and drive off. Harry's attention turned back to the shrubbery concealing the apartment block.

"So, they've been talking to him. I wonder how much they know. And how much has the little rat told them?" Moving swiftly, Harry left the car and hurried towards Jake's apartment.

***

"I've been thinking about what you said." Belinda whisked the eggs and poured them into the omelette pan. "About them all being guilty."

Hazel, fretting over the loss of her couturier garments, not to mention her loss of dignity at the fish pond, hadn't slept well. She replied with a grunt.

"Suppose they are," Belinda continued, "Max had something they wanted, let's say the negative of the old film, so they kept him prisoner until he revealed where it was. Then, in frustration, because he remained silent, they did him in."

"Which means, of course, they reduced their chances of finding the negative," said Hazel as she poured a fresh cup of coffee.

"Which is why Jake broke into the house to

search for it."

"You suspect he wanted to find it first and cut the others out? I wouldn't put it past the little sod," said Hazel.

"And that's why Harry and Charmaine gave him a bad time," said Belinda. "Knowing he'd broken into the house, they thought he had found the negative."

"I imagine this group was not doing this for altruistic reasons. Presumably they could sell this rare item for a lot of money."

"Right," said Belinda thoughtfully. "I think we need to talk to each member and see what their story is."

"The police would have asked all the questions."

Belinda served up the omelettes. "Possibly, but did they get the right answers? Such as why Max was held prisoner and then murdered. What was the motive? My guess is whatever the police discovered is far from the truth."

"We don't know any of these people. How do we make contact with them?"

"Through Bridie. I'll think of a way to pick their brains."

Hazel attacked the omelette. "Well, you do that. I'll have another go with the young turk."

Belinda smiled. "Best wear a wet-suit."

Hazel's response would best be described as uncultured.

***

Belinda watched as Bridie stepped from her car, looked furtively around, and slipped under the police Crime Scene tape securing Max's house. Parked nearby but out of sight, Belinda had followed Bridie's car from the College. It had been her intention to question Bridie there, but on arrival, it was to see her get into a car and drive off. Belinda swiftly turned her car and followed. Dark clouds delivered a downpour, and the windscreen wipers could barely clear the rain, making conditions difficult, so Belinda had trouble keeping her in sight. She assumed Bridie was heading for home and she could talk to her there. Gradually as the rain eased, it became clear they were travelling to the other side of the city. She was uncertain if Bridie was aware she was being tailed and was surprised when her car slowed and stopped outside the murder house.

Belinda left her car nearby and moved to get a more unobstructed view from under the water-logged branches of trees in the park. Bridie was not in sight. Then she appeared catlike from the back of the house, her legs encased in black leggings emerging from beneath an oversized white sweater. This combination gave the impression a large egg was terrorising the neighborhood. Puffing her way to the front door and with another guileful glance, she took a bunch of keys from her tote bag, sorted through them, selected one, and slipped it into the lock. A quick turn. The door opened. Bridie disappeared into the house.

The clouds thickened, and rain began to fall again as Belinda crossed the street and stepped up to the entrance porch. She tested the door. It gave and, with a further push, opened silently to reveal the dark and empty hall. A wave of stagnant and rank air rushed to overwhelm her forcing her to step back and gasp for fresh air.

Recovering, she stepped into the hall. What little light there was from the open door accompanied her for only a few steps before she was forced to reach out for guidance and run her hand along the wall as she progressed. Each pace drew her further into the blackness; the only sound the rainwater gushing down ineffectual pipes.

Eventually, her eyes grew accustomed to the gloom and the faint light from the window in the landing, its colours now muted, indicated the staircase. From up above came the sound of anger and frustration conveyed in raucous exclamations by an enraged female.

Belinda climbed the stairs as the uproar continued. Turning into the first doorway, she was confronted by the sight of large black and white buttocks, which appeared to be stuck under the four-poster bed. Wild sibilant curses confirmed the imprisonment. Belinda bent and grasping the two black legs attached to the backside, dragged the suffering Bridie free. She sat up panting for breath, her voluminous white jumper covered in dust bunnies.

Belinda took a lit torch from her hands, scanned the room, located a bedside lamp, and switched in on, helping to eliminate some of the melancholy atmosphere. Surfaces were covered in a veil of fingerprint powder, evidence that the crime scene officers had done their duty.

Bridie blinked and looked at Belinda in surprise. "What are you doing here?"

"Funny, I was going to ask you the same question," said Belinda, "and you can thank your stars I am, or you would have been stuck under the bed for the foreseeable future.

Bridie gave a petulant shake of her shoulders and began to remove the clinging dust bunnies. "I think I have more of a right to be here than you."

"Possibly. After all, you have the key. I know the police confiscated all the keys, so how is it that you still have one?"

Bridie glared at her, hauled herself up and perched on the unmade bed. "I don't see that it's any of your business, Belinda Lawrence," she said waspishly. "You always were high and mighty, even at school, and now just because you're going to marry some millionaire, you needn't think you can push people around."

Belinda sighed. She had a memory of schoolyard hostility and a plump Bridie, forever on the perimeter of adolescent worldliness. Sullen. Sulky. "You're wrong about the millionaire but right about it being none of my business. Still, the police might think it's *their* business, and when they find out you've got a key to the house, they might begin to put two and two together, and begin to wonder if you tied Max up and eventually killed him."

Bridie's eyes widened, as she stared at Belinda. "You don't think they'd do that, do you?" Her voice had grown thin and croaky. Then she recovered as a thought struck her. "But I was with you that night," she said with superiority. "I collected you and that other woman, Hazel, from your house and drove you here, or had you forgotten that?" She gave a smug smile.

"That's true, you did. But I don't know where you were before you arrived and what you'd been doing. You say the police think Max was murdered only a short time before he was found. How short a time? One hour? Two? Or more? Plenty of time for you to knock him on the head and then collect us as though nothing had happened. You wouldn't have known that Jake was going to break in and find the body."

Once more Bridie looked worried and began to bite on an already ragged fingernail. "I didn't kill him," she whined in a small voice.

"Maybe, "said Belinda, "but let's get back to the key. How did you get one?"

Bridie looked at the floor, avoiding Belinda's eye. "We all had access to the keys. Max gave us one each so we could come and go without bothering him."

"So the police know that? Did they ask?"

Bridie nodded. "I didn't tell them. I don't know about the others. So, when the police took our keys, I'd already had a spare made, which I kept."

Belinda sat down on the bed beside her. "You all knew Max was to be held prisoner?

Bridie nodded. She glanced at Belinda and away again. "Yes. The proposal went wrong, and he got angry and wouldn't agree. So Harry decided to keep him captive until we got what we wanted."

"And what you all wanted was the film of 'Soldiers of the Cross'? Am I right?"

Bridie looked up in surprise. "How...how did you know that?"

"I did my homework," said Belinda, pleased that her suspicions were correct. "You and the others believed Max had the negative to the film segments and they would be worth a lot of money. So what was this 'proposal' you put to him?"

Bridie grimaced. "It all seems so silly now. If the negative for the film was found, it could be sold, and the group wanted a share of it. Harry had heard a rumour about the existence of the film. Max got drunk one night, and Harry asked him if the story was true. Max boasted about how his father the great film entrepreneur had found the film, so Harry suggested to him if the film existed, to sell it and share the money with the group."

"And Max didn't agree?"

"Not only that, he flew into a violent temper. We'd been invited here to the house for drinks. One of his soirees, as he liked to call them. To play the grand host and us to listen to him boast about his father's career as an exhibitor of classic European films. He liked to think he'd inherited the old man's talent as well as his money, but what talent he had was for screening cheap sex and slasher films, and any money came from his marriage. His wife let him very well off.

"Anyway, when Harry made the suggestion, Max turned on him and began to belittle him, called him all sorts of names. Then he said we were all a bunch of losers living in the past, sponging on his hospitality and threatened to close down the group and stop the screenings. He asked for all his keys back. Then he ordered us out of the house. Frankly, I was glad to get away."

"If you all returned your keys to Max…?"

Bridie shrugged. "We had copies made."

Belinda turned her head to look around the room. Dresser drawers had been pulled out, papers, clothing, and books covered the carpet. Nearby, a large wardrobe stood despondently, its doors wide open in submission. "So I gather you were searching under the bed for the missing film?"

"I could see that someone had already searched the room, and the police had been here. I thought maybe they hadn't looked under the bed, and so…" her voice trailed off.

"Have you searched in the murder room?"

"Can't. The police have a security lock on it."

"Let's go back a bit. Max claims to have the missing film. Harry suggests a deal whereby all the group benefits from a sale of the film. Max spits the dummy. At what point was it decided to hold Max prisoner until he agreed to the proposal? So whose scheme was it?"

Chapter Seven

"So as I said, it was Harry who first suggested making Max a prisoner," lisped Jake, as he struggled to open a can of Rum and Cola. Hazel waited for him to continue. Her arrival at his flat had been greeted in the foyer as before with the squeak of a door opposite and through a small gap one watery eye surveying this new activity. The undefinable odour as before, increased as the elderly neighbour, throwing caution to the wind, pushed the door to reveal her full countenance. "I hope you're not going to make a racket like that last visitor he had." Her enraged voice had the ear-splitting characteristic of a cracked Edison Cylinder.

Hazel looked down her nose. "I can assure you I have no intention of playing tennis." This music-hall witticism was lost of the old lady. "Shoutin' and screamin' somethin' shockin'. The language! Effing this and effing that. And the noise and screams! And him with blood all over his face!"

Hazel thought back over this as Jake slaked his thirst, which he did with great difficulty. Swollen and cut lips were a significant impediment. That, two black eyes, bruised cheeks, and a forehead heavily bandaged and bloodstained suggested others. He looks like something Dorian Gray kept in the attic, she thought. "And would I be right in thinking Harry is responsible for your injuries?"

Jake put down the drink and glanced around

the room. "As well as half demolishing the flat," he said thickly.

Hazel was aware the flat would never have featured in Good Housekeeping but the condition it was now in might qualify as a waste disposal site. "That's the second time Harry's roughed you up. Give me your phone number. Next time he calls, ring me." Jake smirked as they exchanged numbers.

"I like that. Wonder Woman protecting me from doctor Mabuse. Will you bring your mate, the Cat Woman with you?"

Hazel ignored the jibe. "I take it he was looking for something?"

Jake grunted. "Took everything apart."

"And he didn't find the negative?"

Jake attempted to smile and pointed at his face. "Does this look like he found it?"

"But he was convinced you had it," said Hazel, "why did he think that?"

Jake took another painful swig of his drink. "It all goes back to when I told him of the possibility of the film existing. Bad move. I should have kept it to myself. He then told the group about his plan to keep Max prisoner until he gave us the negative. He wanted us all to agree, but most of the oldies didn't want to get involved in what they saw as a crime."

"And what about you," said Hazel, "did you agree to hold him prisoner?"

Jake sniggered. "Didn't need to. I already had the negative."

"And Harry knew it?"

"Eventually. Max told him the neg was missing, and Harry put two and two together. He couldn't see the oldies knocking it off, and that young bird and her bloke weren't included in the deal, so suspicion fell on me.

"It was easy enough to find. Max usually got pissed at night and fell asleep, so I had plenty of time to search the house. I'd go there with some DVD's of old films and let him ramble on about the 'old days' and keep topping up his glass until he passed out. He had this really old VHS video camera and made me film him, 'for posterity' he said, and he rambled on about his father being a showman and a great cinema pioneer and how he had carried on his father's work. All bull most of it, but there must have been over ten of those tapes. It was on one of them that he spilled his guts about the 'Soldiers of the Cross' negative. I found it easy enough. Want to see it?"

Hazel looked surprised. "You have it here?"

Jake eased himself out of his chair and kicking his way through the magazines and items that covered the floor, he went to a corner of the room and lifted aside a small cabinet. Kneeling down, he pulled back the worn carpet and eased a section of a floorboard free. He reached down and felt around to bring to the surface a package wrapped in a plastic shower curtain.

Placing it on the floor in front of Hazel he tore aside the covering, revealing a rusty and battered square metal container.

"I've had it for about a month. I'd stand back if I were you. The fumes can be a bit toxic. Are you ready to see what the group believes will make their fortune?" said Jake.

Hazel leaned forward in anticipation anxious to see the mythical treasure.

Jake lifted the lid, and Hazel found herself staring at a reddish brown, solid mass of film welded together, covered in rust coloured dust, and emitting a pungent noxious odour.

***

Lance Benson dished out the cat food, immune to the carnivores twisting and turning in anticipation around his ankles. His thoughts were elsewhere. Why did those two women want to see him? He dropped the empty can into the waste bin. The cats ignored him now. He had served his purpose. Later they would permit him to stroke them and they would be subservient – or give that impression. Lance moved to the window of his cottage in the retirement village. Several residents passed by; some to the library, some to the resident doctor, others to join a bus for a day outing. There was a moment of calm.

Then he saw them approaching through the rose garden. What were their names again? Belinda? Haley? No...Hazel. He switched on the electric kettle and dropped teabags into a teapot. The door chimes, in crude imitation of Big Ben's grandeur, announced the arrival of his visitors.

As they took their seats, Belinda and Hazel came under the critical gaze of the cats, perched now high on a bookcase. They had a splendid view of the intruders.

"When Bridie rang and said you both wanted to see me, I couldn't help wondering why," said Lance, as he passed them mugs of tea. "I mean, why would you want to get mixed up in a murder when you had nothing to do with Max or the group?"

"Believe me, we'd rather not be mixed up, but as we were there when Max's body was found, the police naturally consider us, along with you and the others, as potential killers, so if we can name the murderer, it's to our advantage," said Belinda.

Hazel looked at the milky tea and with some reservation put the unused mug on a coffee table. The cats followed this movement with keen eyes. "Look at it from our point of view," said Hazel, "we are invited out to see a film and end up under suspicion of murder."

Lance considered this and nodded slowly. "Point taken. So, what do you want to ask me?" He pushed away some out-dated copies of '21st Century Cats' from a chair and sat opposite the women.

"Bridie tells me you all had keys to the house," said Belinda.

"True. When the group first started, Max gave each one of us a key. It was to have easy access to his film store, the room he was murdered in. It meant we could select any film he had without bothering him."

"But Jake had to break in."

"Jake was a latecomer. He's only been with the group a short time, and I guess Max forgot to give him a key or didn't want him to have one."

"We know about the plan to keep Max prisoner," said Belinda.

Lance frowned. "Yes. That was Harry's idea. I was against it, as most of the others were as well. He thought he could force Max to hand over the negative of an early Australian film."

"We know about the missing film," said Belinda.

Lance gave a knowing smile. "Bridie?"

"Partly," said Belinda, "but I'd done some research and reached that conclusion. 'Soldiers of the Cross'."

Lance looked meditatively at his tea. After a pause, he said, "The idea was for us to share in the sale of the negative, which as you probably know, was rare and therefore worth a lot of money. That is if Max ever had it or if it even existed."

"Oh, I can assure you, Max had it. And it exists," said Hazel. Lance leaned forward, his excited eyes fixed on her.

"Or rather," continue Hazel, "what remains of it."

Lance blinked and with a deep sigh, sat back into his chair. "Hocky puck," he said softly.

The two women exchanged glances. "Hocky what?" asked Belinda.

"Hocky puck. That's the last stage of nitrate decay."

"I know about that," said Hazel, with a superior smirk. "Old nitrate movie film. It was highly inflammable and dangerous. Started fires in cinemas all the time until safety film was invented. Apart from bursting into flames it also deteriorated if not stored correctly and would rot away, get sticky, and end up a solid block. And believe me, it would stink."

Lance raised a quizzical eyebrow. "You're very knowledgeable?"

"Jake told me," said Hazel in a matter-of-fact manner.

Belinda and Hazel watched his reaction. "So Jake has the negative?" said Lance.

"Had it for some weeks, he says."

"And that's why Harry bashed him up. He must have suspected he had it," said Belinda.

Lance looked startled. "He bashed him? But why would he suspect Jake?"

"Well, he did break into Max's house," said Hazel.

"But you say Jake claims he had the negative for some weeks before the time of Max's murder," mused Lance.

"What were you doing on the day of the murder?" asked Belinda.

A shadow of irritation passed over Lance's face. "I've been all through this with the police. I called into our little theatre earlier in the day. I'd left a film there from a previous screening and wanted to collect it in case it went missing."

"Did you see anyone else there?"

"No. Although, I thought I saw Harry's car turn into the street as I was leaving, I couldn't be sure it was his. Harry, of course, denies being anywhere near the house."

"But that was early in the day. What about later?"

Lance frowned in annoyance. "I've told the police what my movements were. I see no reason to tell you, except to say I didn't return to the house at any stage until the evening for the screening." He was silent for a moment. "So if the negative has decayed, Harry's scheme to make money from it has collapsed."

"And Max was murdered for nothing," said Belinda, "but it still makes the group potential killers. And that includes you." The inference created a tension in the room. The cats leapt from the bookcase and sat staring at the two intruders.

Lance looked Belinda in the eye. "Yes. Yes, it does include me."

As they walked away from the cottage, Belinda and Hazel felt accusing eyes burning into their backs. Four feline. Two human.

"If it is true that Jake had the negative for several weeks," said Belinda, "it raises the question –"

"- why did he break into the house, and what was he searching for at the time Max was killed," concluded Hazel.

Chapter Eight

Harry angrily threw his mobile phone across the room. It bounced off the wall, knocked a photo of Sylvester Stallone sideways and landed with the sound of something shattering among glasses on the drinks cabinet. "The little rat!" The phone call from Lance telling him the news the negative had decayed and was of no value to the group enraged him. At that moment that fury was directed against Jake who, it seems, had known all along the film was worthless. To calm himself and have time to think he poured a Scotch, neat, and lit a cigarette. So if the kid had found the negative, realised it was of no value, what was he doing breaking into Max's house? Was there something else of value that he was going to steal and not tell the group? Perhaps another visit to Jake was due. And maybe a repeat of his last visit. Only this time even more violent. Meanwhile, he'd better let the others know the bad news. He crossed the room and picked up his phone. Battered and bruised it seemed to have survived his violence. He began to type in a text message.

***

Charmaine scanned the text message. She gave a snort of rage. Gone. All gone. All her plans... Well, she agreed with Harry. That child ought to be taught a lesson. A real lesson this time. Losing Max was one thing...actually losing his money had been the more significant loss if she was being honest with herself. So the prospect of a share in the sale of the valuable film would have been some compensation. Now even that had gone. If only the stupid boy had told them about the negative being useless. He'd had it for some weeks. Weeks before Max died.

And if he hadn't died, she could have been... She glanced at her watch. Harry said, 'in an hour'. At the usual place. She gathered up her coat, set the security lock, and took the lift down to the foyer. She wondered what Harry had in mind. Revenge?

***

Bridie plummeted heavily into her office chair and snarled at a student who dropped a newly edited social documentary DVD on her desk. (The Modern Woman. What is she?) "Late as usual, Melanie. Just leave it there. I'll look at it later. If I consider it being worth the effort." Melanie knew better than to argue with Miss Kelly when she was in that mood and crept noiselessly out to tell her mates that 'Old Mother Kelly's' was having her scheduled maintenance and it was wise to stay out of her way.

Bridie's ill-temper had nothing to do with any physical condition; her indisposition was mental, although it could be said her blood pressure had risen alarmingly, and abnormal thoughts of torture and impalement shared company with bloodletting in her unusually active brain.

So, the negative had been found and was useless. And discovered by that obnoxious creep, Jake. She'd never liked him. When he found out she ran the film school, he poked fun at her and said you couldn't learn filmmaking from a school. You learned by watching films.

Well, maybe that was partly true. But to know he had the negative and hadn't told anyone. She wondered why? Did he know something else about the film? Her anger rose again, and she whimsically mimed slitting his throat from ear to ear. Sadly this did nothing to alleviate her rage. Rage because although the money gained from selling the film would have been nice, it was the kudos she would have received from the Arts and Film world as someone who found this lost national treasure. That was to have been her crowning glory and an entree into the REAL film world. Visions of being applauded on the red carpet the Cannes Film Festival; rubbing shoulders with Nicole and Cate; being invited to speak at the Film Society of Lincoln Centre, all shattering to reveal her bleak future bounded by pooped out schoolrooms. She glanced at her watch. She was due in the theatrette for a screening of an early Jack Thompson film, SILO 15. She'd get someone else to take the class; right now she needed to express her anger physically, and you can only go so far in taking it out on a roomful of pestilential students.

***

June Allyson was just finishing a big production number, 'Thou Swell, Thou Witty, Thou Graaannnd' as Muriel switch off the Video player. Joe looked up at her in astonishment. "It seems the missing negative has been found and is no good," she said, as she placed a battered black hat on her grey hair. It rested there like a flat gloomy burnt omelette.

Joe, still immersed in MGM extravagance, was bewildered and it took a moment for her words to sink in. "No good?"

"Yes, rotted away. You know what that means?" Joe didn't but gave a nod.

Muriel continued, "It means we won't be sharing in any money that would have come from the sale of the film, and that means no repairs to the house." She was struggling into an overall smock and buttoning up the front. Next, her coat, and finally pulling on fine leather gloves. Joe smiled. He'd given her the gloves on their tenth wedding anniversary. He'd had to buy men's gloves, because she had such big hands. "I'm going out for a while and not sure what time I'll be back." She gathered up her bag, walked to the bathroom, opened the medicine cabinet and took a selection of pills. She hesitated, then reached in for another item.

As she returned to Joe, he was fiddling with the Video player. She handed him some pills. "If I'm not back by teatime, remember to take one of these before you eat."

"Where are you going?"

"Just out."

"You always say that, 'just out'. You never tell me where."

Muriel sighed and bent to kiss him on the head. "As if you'd remember? Just the usual tasks. You know I have to do odd jobs. Our pension doesn't go far enough. Now go on and enjoy your film."

She closed the door softly behind her, and he heard her footsteps fade away. The video was playing again, so he settled back as June appeared on the screen. 'Thy words are queer, Sir, unto mine ear, Sir.'

***

Another interview with the police and more questioning took up most of the next day. The questioning mainly centred about their knowledge of the members of the Society, but as Hazel acerbically reminded the interviewing officer, she was visiting the country and was not accustomed to mixing with cinematic octogenarians of any nationality. Belinda echoed her previous answers on her childhood friendship with Bridie, and it was only by chance they had met up again, and she could tell them little about the group. Nothing seemed to be achieved from the interview, but they were assured that their DNA was not found in the murder room, whereas it seems that wasn't the case with the Society members; DNA from each one tallied with that found at the murder scene.

In an attempt to put the murder out of their

minds the two women visited ACMI, watched an Australian film, had a coffee and wandered into the 'Screen Worlds The Story of Film, Television & Digital Culture' exhibition. Belinda reflected that it was here that she'd met Bridie and the whole murderous episode had unravelled. She pointed out the coloured stills used in the film, 'Soldiers of the Cross' but Hazel showed more interest in the collection of old movie cameras and television paraphernalia. This included early home movie Video Cameras that used VHS tapes. She nudged Belinda. "Remember Jake told me that he'd taped Max on an old camera?"

Belinda took out her compact and studied her makeup. "Yes. So what?"

"Well, apparently the camera used VHS tapes, and they could still be in the old house."

Belinda snapped the compact shut. "Probably. But why the interest?"

"Jake said there were a number of tapes, ten or so. Suppose he broke into the house to find the tapes. If he knew the negative of the film was no good, maybe there was something on one of the tapes that related to the missing film."

"And he came across Max's body before he found them," said Belinda, thoughtfully.

They made their way from Federation Square and climbed the stairs at nearby Young and Jackson's pub where drinkers had been quenching their thirst since 1861. Seated beneath the painting of a nude Chloe, the young French model who had scandalised Victorian Melbourne, Hazel gratefully quaffed a healthy swig of her gin & tonic; Belinda settled for white wine. She sighed. "I suppose by now, Lance has told all the other members of the group the negative has rotted away."

"Which won't please Harry," said Hazel.

"Your theory that Jake was looking for some VHS tapes is interesting," Belinda said, "of course he could have been looking for a number of things. A film. Money. Valuables."

"No," said Hazel, "my gut feeling is for the tapes. Suppose Max revealed something about the film. Jake remembered this, and he wanted to get his hands on them again."

"But with the negative useless, what could it be?"

Hazel gave an indecisive shrug. "We could always ask him." She took out her mobile phone and punched in a number. While waiting for an answer, she gazed at the painting of Cloe. "Pretty little thing. Who was she?"

"Marie. Only nineteen. She was an artist's model in Paris. Painted by a Jules Lefebvre as Chloe. Later she concocted a soup made from match heads. Drank the poison, made up of sulphur and other things, and died. Unrequited love, they say."

Hazel grunted. "It'll get you every time." She switched off the phone. "No answer. Jake might be scared Harry is calling him. Let's drop in on him on the way home."

***

Twilight once again reduced the garden at Jake's apartment block to a place of secrets and unease. There was no sign of life as they approached the building. Entering, they expected to be challenged by the old woman in the flat opposite, but all was silent. An eerie silence. Belinda shivered. Jake's door was ajar. Belinda pushed it aside. The room was dark with only a faint light filtering in from the open door.

"Jake. Are you there?" called Belinda.

There was no answer. "Let's go in," said Hazel brushing past. She switched on a reading lamp.

Jake lay on the couch. "He's asleep," said Hazel as she went to wake him. Belinda grasped her arm. "No. Don't touch him. Look." Hazel followed Belinda's gaze.

On the floor beside Jake were a small candle, a spoon, and a hypodermic needle. His arm hung down, and blood had trickled onto the floor. Belinda stepped closer and felt his arm. It was cold. Cold as ice. She drew her hand away in revulsion. "He's dead."

"And we don't have a roast onion," whispered Hazel as she stared at the pale corpse.

Belinda frowned at her. "What did you say?

Hazel shook her head as though to clear it. "Nothing. I was just... I'll tell you later."

Belinda reached for her phone. "We need to call the police."

Chapter Nine

Belinda felt she was becoming over-familiar with the Interrogation Room at Police Headquarters where, in separate rooms, she and Hazel were providing a written report and answering questions about Jake's death. Hazel reported her previous meeting with Jake, how he said had been bashed by Harry and revealed the old film negative was decayed. So if the police hadn't known about the plan for the group to profit from the sale of the film, they did now. Finally, after giving more DNA samples, they were released pending further questioning, and as they made their way out of the building, Hazel said, "I didn't mention the VHS tapes. Should I have told them?"

"That's only a theory we have. No use to them at this stage. If we do discover anything of interest, that'll be the time to pass on the information," said Belinda. A stocky man in a hurry brushed past them. Belinda recognised him.

"That's Sam. Remember we met him the night Max was murdered." She ran after him and clutched his arm. Surprised, he stopped and turned to her. "Sam? I'm sorry to startle you. You may remember me?"

Sam gave a half-smile. "Right. Yes, I do. The night...the night Max..."

"Yes, the night he died. We'd come with Bridie to see a film."

Hazel joined them. "I'm Belinda," continued Belinda, "and this is Hazel."

Another half-smile as Sam acknowledged them both. "Have you been interrogated too?" he said. "I've never had any contact with police before, well certainly not about a murder. Really cool, don't you think?"

"Chilling," said Belinda, dryly. "Look, is there a coffee shop around here where we can talk. We've fallen into this murder – or rather what seems to be two murders - and would like to get some information about the group."

Sam glanced around and then again, the half-smile. "Actually my studio is only a ten-minute walk from here. Why not go there?"

Belinda looked at Hazel who gave a frown. To Sam, "Thanks. That sounds ideal. Lead the way." As they set off behind his strong figure, Hazel hissed in her ear, "You realise he could be the murderer."

"We'll just have to chance it," replied Belinda, showing bravura she didn't really feel.

The studio was down a small alleyway and contained within remains of a dilapidated warehouse. Sections of the open floor space were designated as various quarters; a living room complete with a worn settee and a coffee table, crowded in by looming bookshelves laden with a potpourri of literary and libidinous tracts. A corner had been appropriated as sleeping quarters evidenced by a double bed partly hidden by a scarlet coverlet which failed to cover crumpled pyjamas, and a large orange cat was viewing the new arrivals with some malice.

There appeared to be a kitchen behind a screen which Sam disappeared into to make coffee, after inviting Belinda and Hazel to take a seat on the settee, which they did with some reservations. It seems the screen also hid a toilet as the sound of a flushing cistern caused both women to hope Sam was in the habit of washing his hands.

As startling as this mise en scène was, it cowered under the presence of hundreds of photographs lining the walls; old silent film stars some small, some large, Chaplin, Garbo, Harold Lloyd, Douglas Fairbanks, Rudolph Valentino, Lillian Gish, William S Hart, Agnes Dobson, Lottie Lyell and many others that time has erased from cinematic memories. Across the room shelves of film cans clung to the wall, while before them was a bench with various implements which they assumed had to do with film production. Hazel rose and inspected the bench. "What do you use this for?"

Sam's head poked out from behind the screen. "That's where I rewind and repair my films."

Hazel picked up a heavy metal item which had a handle on a hinge, and a sharp blade. "And this?"

"That's a film splicer or tape splicer. You join two pieces of film together with sticky tape."

As Hazel went to replace the splicer, it slipped from her fingers and landed, painfully, on her toes, the sharp edges digging into her flesh. She gave a yelp.

Sam hurried for behind the screen. "Be careful. I don't want to break that. It cost me a lot." He picked up the splicer and scrutinized it carefully.

"I doubt it will break. It's too solid. Not like my poor toes," said Hazel sharply as she sat beside Belinda and massaged the damaged foot.

"I must remember to loan it to the group, that is if there's still going to be a group. The splicer in the projection room went walkabout. Max probably took it out of spite. He was always doing things like that. Strange bloke. Blew hot and cold. One day all over you, the next didn't want to know you."

The brew proved to be of the instant variety and both women, after a tentative sip, left their coffee on the table to decompose. Sam sat opposite them in a sagging deck chair taking large gulps of his beverage, his eyes flicking from one to the other.

Belinda broke the silence. "Did you have an alibi for the day Max was murdered?"

"Yes. I told the police. I spent most of the day at a small cinema in Carlton. I often help out there; makes me feel I'm still part of the biz. I came in on the last days of screening films so really don't have that much experience, and I don't like digital." He leaned forward, some excitement in his speech. "Do you know it's all an illusion?"

"What is?" snapped Hazel, who was beginning to wish they'd never come.

"Film. The eye retains an image for a fraction of a second which allowed the projector to pull down the next frame, which replaces the retained image with a fresh one, and so on. Without the eye retaining the image, we wouldn't have films." This was obviously something that he found fascinating and magical.

Belinda, fearing he would continue in this vein said, "Back to Max. On that day did you go to his house at all?"

"No, not to his house. I called into his theatrette on the way to Carlton."

"Why?" asked Hazel.

Sam glanced at her. He didn't like her very much. She reminded him of his ex-wife; pushy and domineering. "I don't see it has anything to do with you, but I wanted to collect a book I'd left there. A book on silent films." He gestured to the pictures on the wall. "It's a sort of hobby of mine. The book was very old and valuable, and I didn't want to lose it. I was only there for a few minutes."

"Did you see anyone else?" said Belinda.

Sam frowned. "I'm not sure. I thought I heard someone in the garden. When I looked, I caught a glimpse of someone as they disappeared around the corner of the house."

"And you couldn't recognise them?"

Sam shook his head. "By the time I got outside they'd disappeared."

"And what about yesterday?" said Hazel. "What about Jake?"

Sam once again frowned. "Well, I was home here all day. I told the police I didn't know where he lived but whether they believe me or not - I had no alibi, so I suppose they could think it was me that gave Jake a Hot Shot".

"A hot what?"

"A Hot Shot. Didn't you know?" Sam suddenly felt superior to these women. "Oh yes. I wheedled it out of a mate of mine, one of the cops at headquarters. Yes. A massive overdose of heroin."

"An overdose? But he could have given himself that," said Belinda.

"Maybe, but it's usually given when you want to kill someone."

The cat leapt off the bed and sashayed across the room to a litter tray which Hazel hadn't noticed. It was quite near her feet. Here, the cat, giving Hazel a look of satanic pleasure, passed a comment on the conversation. Following this, it was generally agreed the meeting had come to an end.

On the tram a short time later as they made their way home to East Melbourne, Hazel said, "How do we know he got the information about the hot shot injection from a cop? Maybe he gave Jake the injection himself."

Belinda looked thoughtful. "OK. Two murders. But one - or two - murderers?"

***

"Harry's been taken into custody on suspicion of Max's murder and charged with unlawful imprisonment, as well as giving Jake an overdose. They found his DNA in Jake's flat along with

Charmaine's." Bridie paused for breath.

"That'd be from the time they roughed him up, if not his murder," said Hazel.

Giving her a questioning glance, Bridie continued, "He's out on bond over the imprisonment, the other suspicions can't be proved, at least not just now, and his movements restricted to Melbourne. And the coroner has released Max's body for burial." Bridie, gasping for breath, collapsed into a chair. Her early arrival in the role of Hermes at Belinda's house, found both women luxuriating over their morning coffee. They absorbed this news fresh from the law enforcement nerve centre. Belinda was on her hands and knees connecting a power lead which was attached to a 'seen better days' VHS player. Hazel was searching through a collection of VHS tapes, mostly old black and white films of the forties and an occasional musical.

Having regained some composure, Bridie prattled on. "The body's been released to Max's solicitor, and he's arranging the funeral. That's because there's no family. Then there will be a cremation and the ashes scattered."

"So he's not been charged with the murders? Harry, I mean," said Belinda as she stood upright and took a sip of coffee.

Still short of breath, Bridie shook her head. She swallowed and said, "I can see why they'd suspect him of killing Max, after all, he was the one who planned to keep him prisoner... but I don't know how they made a connexion with Jake's overdose. After all, Harry had nothing to do with the boy. Couldn't stand him, as far as I know."

Belinda and Hazel looked at each other. "Are they sure Jake didn't give himself the injection?" said Belinda.

Bridie gave a noncommittal shrug. She eyed the coffee pot. Typical of 'Lady of the Manor', Belinda not to offer a guest a cup of coffee. Belinda, as though reading her thoughts said, "Would you like a coffee?"

Bridie gave an ungracious sniff. "No thanks." She gave a glance around the room. Hazel had selected a VHS tape. "Bel, try this and see if the machine is still working. She handed the tape to Belinda and switched on the TV set.

Bridie gave a snigger. Hazel looked at her. "What's so funny?"

Bridie gestured at the tape. "The Sound of Music? Surely you're not going to watch that? Robert Wise, a good director in his day, but Julie Andrews? Really."

Hazel took a threatening step towards her. "Somethin' wrong with Julie Andrews?" The permafrost in Hazel's voice convinced Bridie she was on thin ice, so she rapidly searched for salvation. "Oh, I must tell you. Muriel says after the funeral we should have a wake in Max's memory."

Belinda turned to her. "A wake?"

"Yes, you know, like the Irish. A celebration of his life."

"And where does Muriel expect to hold the

wake?"

"Well, in the old house. Seeing Max lived and died there, and he used to have his soirees there, so it was thought the ideal place. Muriel says she will see to the catering."

Belinda and Hazel both nodded. "I think that's a splendid idea, "said Belinda. She turned to the VHS player and switched it on. After a few grunts and groans, Julie appeared on the TV screen in full flight amidst hills alive with music. Bridie gave a groan, struggled from her chair and backed towards the door. "Well, I'll be going." But there was no response. She slipped out the door. Belinda glanced up from the TV set to see her scuttling away towards the Treasury Gardens. She switched off the VHS player. "Well, we know it still works, and we can see Max's tapes - when and if we find them."

"Hazel nodded, "And we'll have the perfect opportunity to search for them during Max's wake."

***

Harry stepped down from the entrance to the police headquarters. His usual sprightliness had deserted him. Several hours of interrogation had punctured the armour of vainglory he'd forged for himself. His lawyer had got him out on a bond for the unlawful imprisonment charge. He'd never had to justify his actions to any man, but an explanation was demanded by the law, and his dexterity in convincing them he was innocent of the murders of Max and

Jake had tested his cunning and ingenuity. It seemed to have paid off as he was now released from the arms of the law, due to insufficient evidence. He glanced across the street where Charmaine stood waiting by a taxi. Standing erect and with some theoretical bravura he forced himself into the role of dominant male and crossed the road.

Charmaine greeted him with an attempted embrace which he shook off and climbed into the back seat of the taxi. Bewildered, Charmaine sat beside him. She glanced at his face. It was white and his jaw tense. She wondered what he was thinking.

If she could read his thoughts, he was thinking - was it enough for Charmaine to have perjured herself and claimed on the night of Jake's murder, he had been with her at her apartment watching TV. He hadn't of course, but would the cops be able to trace his movement that night? And now he owed Charmaine. What was it called? 'Bearing false witness?' She'd put herself at risk by lying for him, and he didn't like to be beholden to any man – or woman. He'd have to play along with her now. If she turned nasty, she could drop him in it. She put her hand on his knee and gave an affectionate squeeze, no doubt to show her sympathy. He reluctantly took her hand in his and held it limply. But he didn't look at her; stared straight ahead into the back of the driver's neck. The man could do with a haircut.

The drive took them through the start of the evening peak traffic. After a long slow journey, they eventually arrived at Charmaine's apartment block. As she alighted, she turned to Harry. "Are you coming in?" Harry pulled the taxi door closed and spoke through the open window. "No. I'll call you later."

Charmaine stepped back as the taxi took off. Fumbling with her keys, she entered the foyer and pressed the lift button. Why was Harry being so aloof? She wondered what alibi he had offered to police regarding Max's murder. He'd asked her to vouch for him being with her the night Jake was killed. She'd readily agreed, firstly because she didn't think he'd committed the crime, and secondly... why secondly?

The lift door opened and she entered to be whisked up to her floor. Her apartment seemed like a calm sanctuary after the confusion and tension of the police headquarters and all the never-ending questioning. She sank down on the sofa. The strain of Max's murder, followed by Jake's, sat heavily on her shoulders. The police thought someone in the group had to be the murderer. But who? Did they suspect her? Did they believe her when she said she couldn't have murdered Max because she... what had she told them? A mental fog descended, and she fought to regain her thoughts. Oh, yes. She'd been shopping in the city. She hadn't of course and had no evidence to back up her claim so the police would suggest she'd had plenty of time to visit Max and murder him. But so had Harry, and he certainly did bash Jake up. Could he have gone too far? She wondered about the others in the group. What alibis for both murders did they have? If any.

***

Joe fiddled discontentedly with a battered nineteen-forty film fan magazine. The police had asked him strange questions. It seems Old Max was dead. Murdered. And the police asked strange questions. What was he doing on the night of the murder? Before the screening. Probably watching Two Girls and a Sailor with June. He had to explain who June Allyson was to these infantile policemen. Some of them women! His mind wandered. And pretty little Gloria de Haven. No. Back to the present. Why would they think he'd kill Max? Or anyone? That young lad, Jack? Jake. He died too. Joe shivered. He didn't like what was happening. He hoped Muriel would be home soon from her job. He'd feel safe then.

***

Muriel took off her hat and coat and undid her work pinny. Joe was dozing in front of the TV set. She bent and kissed him on the top of his head. He stirred but dozed off again. She knew the police interrogation has fazed him and in his bewildered state had sought her comforting eyes. But he had been alone and gave garbled answers. Plainly they could see that he was harmless and wouldn't hurt a fly. She'd told them she'd been at the group's cinema to deliver a sponge cake for the evening's screening. She was vague about what time of day that was; some time after lunch. Max had been murdered about three or four hours before they found him. Had she seen anyone else at the house? She'd told them 'no'. But did they believe her?

***

The coffin containing the mortal remains of Maximilian de Lautour, film exhibitor, bon vivant, raconteur, and general all-around pain in the neck, bore no ornamentation to indicate therein rested a self-proclaimed giant of the cinema, or indeed that of a victim of a recent murder. No doubt gloomy cosmeticians had made futile attempts to reconstruct his face but had to settle for a generic 'one face fits all' before the coffin lid was mercifully screwed down. On the surface, it appeared the world had finished with Max de Lautour, but that was far from the truth. The funeral parlour was as bleak as the coffin, apart from some dusty plastic lilies failing in their duty to express sympathy or a suggestion of all things ethereal. The room was bare although some chairs were arranged to face a blank wall, while the deceased was shunted off to the side, out of view and almost an afterthought.

A piercing squeak not unlike the last trump reverberated as Belinda and Hazel opened the door and entered. All the heads of the mourners turned in unison to vet the new arrivals.

"All the usual suspects," muttered Hazel, as

they took their place in the back row.

The suspects included Harry and Charmaine, Muriel and Joe, Lance, Sam. Completing the silent mourners a few white-haired men given to fondling ambulatory appliances, and an elderly woman with barbaric makeup, seemingly applied by an unsteady trowel beneath an over-elaborate hairstyle.

"Probably other old projectionists who knew Max, and the woman I bet was an usherette," whispered Belinda.

"And her wig is something from the chamber of horrors," Hazel whispered back. They both turned their eyes to the two tall men standing at the back of the room. No need to guess their identity. 'Cops.' The unspoken acknowledgment was transmitted in the glances the two women exchanged.

Apart from an occasional cough or the creaking of a chair, as a griever shifted from one buttock to the other in the hard seats, the silence was harrowing. More than one began to wonder why they had come and when, if ever, something would happen. In answer to their discomfort, a wraith-like figure in the form of a willowy funeral director appeared as if from nowhere and stood before them.

"Dear people," he breathed softly, which caused those with hearing aids to check their efficacy while other strained forward in their seats lest they miss the next act in what, to some, was taking on the appearance of a non-event. "The late Mr de Lautour," continued the director, "indicated that he wanted a simple service among friends. So I invite any of you who have memories of our late departed brother and wish to share them with us, you are welcome to do so now." He glanced fearfully and discouragingly over the top of his glasses. Two of the grey-haired men rose at the same time and after disentangling their walkers both gave extremely unfunny incidents they had witnessed during their time with Max, and having stood for fully five minutes felt that was enough time to spend on him (their backs and legs were about to give way) staggered back to their seats in a state of collapse.

The usherette swayed to the front and for the next ten minutes told much of her own life with only an occasional mention of Max, and it was just the restraining hand of the wraith who took her arm and guided her back to her seat, that averted a noisy incident. He gave a nod, and two funeral attendants materialised near the coffin.

"As we farewell our brother, please all stand to send him on his way," moaned the director. There was a clamour of creaking, protesting bones, as the group stood. As the attendants placed their hands on the mortuary trolley, the piercing squeak of the last trump filled the room again as a late arrival opened the door. All heads turned again in unison. Two young people dressed in hiking gear stood before them.

Belinda's eyes opened wide in surprise. "It's Tommy and Adele." While the mourners were distracted, Max was unceremoniously pushed through the side door.

***

"But we don't know what Harry's movements were on the day Max was murdered," said Belinda. She and Hazel were preparing to go to Max's wake. Lipstick applied. A spray of perfume here...there. "Should we have worn black?"

Hazel looked at her in the mirror where she'd been examining her features for cunning wrinkles. "Let's not get carried away. Remember we aren't so much mourning Max, as planning to search his house. Besides, black before sunset is rather calculating, don't you think?"

"Well, this afternoon does provide us with the opportunity you mentioned, but it's also the first time the group has been together and gives us a chance to observe them in their natural environment."

"So what do we know, so far? Muriel, who is supplying a gastronomic feast for us today, delivered a sponge cake on the afternoon of the murder. No one saw her, so she had time to bop Max on the head."

"True. But Lance visited the cinema and thought he saw Harry car nearby."

"Right. Sam says he collected a book and thought he saw someone in the garden, but couldn't identify who it was.

"We don't know about Harry or Charmaine. It will be interesting to hear their story, and what they told the police."

"If Harry has been released due to lack of evidence, he must have spun them a convincing tale." Convinced now that the errant wrinkles had been held at bay for one more day, Hazel tossed the car keys to Belinda. "Here, you drive. I've some thinking to do."

Belinda gave a shiver. "It's getting cold. Winter's coming. Time for something warm to wear and that house will be like an icebox. She sorted through her wardrobe and selected a snug fitting herringbone tweed jacket. Suitably attired she led the way to the car, and they drove off.

"This 'thinking' you have to do. What is it?" asked Belinda as she kept an eye on a group of cyclists.

"Well firstly, if we are to search for the VHS tapes, how do we plan to excuse ourselves from the group?"

Belinda smiled." I could ask to go to the bathroom."

"You'd probably get away with it once, but hardly twice or more."

"I could always say I have a weak bladder. And what excuse could you give?"

"I'm thinking of 'a stranger in town' and fascinated by Melbourne's gold rush past. The house being built in that era etc., etc., so to me it is fascinating."

"Do you think they'll buy that?"

"I'll give it a damn good go." She glanced out the window. "Why do cyclists insist on wearing that dreadful skin-tight lycra and covering themselves in advertising like so many bulbous billboards?"

Belinda smiled and stopped the car at a red light. "The other thing of interest is the reappearance of Tom and his girl, Adele."

Hazel started and pointed at a beauty parlour. "Talk of the devil, isn't that Adele coming out of 'Zip & Zing Beauticians'?"

Belinda looked. "Yes, it is. If she's been hiking she probably needed a scrub up."

The lights changed to green, and they drove on. "Hmmm," mused Hazel, "Our own Ken and Barbie. "If we are to suspect them of killing Max, we have to find a motive."

"Jake said they didn't know about the missing film, remember?" said Belinda.

"He '*said*'. But what if he was wrong? I gather they knew little about the group and clearly Jake didn't have much time for them, so Harry could have involved them in the scheme without Jake knowing."

"OK, let's assume they knew of it, what would have driven them to murder?"

Chapter Ten

Muriel placed a plate of sausage rolls on a table already displaying her culinary skills; several sponge cakes fought for space with sandwiches and four types of dips. Lamingtons and Vanilla Slices, those stalwarts of Aussie cuisine that had sustained the nation through two World Wars and beyond, dominated the repast. Four bottles of passionless wine awaited disappointed palates. "The young ones, Tommy and Adele, aren't coming," Muriel said to Belinda.

"Probably don't want any more to do with a murder," said Belinda as she reached for an egg and cress sandwich. She and Hazel had joined the group in the Garden Room of the old house.

Muriel paused in rearranging some of the dishes and looked reflective. "I suppose so. Being young, death is something inconceivable to them, so when faced with the reality, they shrink back in denial." She cast an amused glance at Belinda. "And I don't mean that great Egyptian river."

Belinda smiled at her attempt at humour. "But what about you? You don't seem that distressed?"

"Well, death is part of the job, if you know what I mean."

Belinda couldn't think of any reply and looked around the room. Other members of the group were seated or standing in the green tangle of ferns, Bromeliads, and Glory Vine, all plants looking a little worse for wear. Hazel was talking to Harry. Charmaine, resembling an aged Nymph of the West in the mythological garden of Hesperides, was seated nearby among the ferns and watching them closely.

"Harry, I hear the police released you for want of evidence," said Hazel.

Harry glanced at her, took a sip of his wine, grimaced and tipped the remainder into a pot plant. "I see you've been listening to the grapevine."

"Possibly. But what evidence were they looking for? Your movements on the day Max were murdered?"

Harry was silent and gazed out the window. Hazel continued. "It seems almost the entire group had cause to be at the house at some time that day. But you?"

Harry turned and glared at her. "I've told the police my movements, and I'm damned if I have to tell *you*."

"True, but at least one of the group thought they saw your car in the street. Why would it be in the street unless you were going to the house?"

"Whoever said they saw the car was mistaken-"

"Or lying," said Hazel sharply.

Harry was silent for a moment. "That's possible."

"So if it was a lie, was it to protect them, or to put the blame on you?"

Hazel was aware that the group had ceased

talking amongst themselves and were listening keenly to her conversation. Belinda and Muriel had edged closer to the others. Charmaine rose from the underbrush. "Harry was with me. Both times. On the day Max died and when Jake was killed." There was defiance in her speech and manner. A short silence. Harry turned his back on Hazel. The others slowly resumed their chatter only to be silenced again with the unexpected arrival of two more mourners.

"Congratulate us. We've just got married." Tommy and Adele stood in the doorway, both beaming complacent smiles. This could have been deduced by their dress, the hiking gear of the morning had been replaced by more formal attire: a smart suit for Tommy with boutonnière. A bunch of violets clutched by Adele with some conviction served as a wedding bouquet, while a simple white silk dress bore witness to her married state. Hazel's familiarity with haute couture (she had Givenchy on her speed dial) recognised the cut and styling of a master designer, and that meant 'money'. How did this seemingly average young woman lay her hands on such subdued opulence?

The stunned group slowly came to life, and faint mutters of congratulations filled the air before it returned to its state of disinterest. Hazel took two glasses of wine to the newlyweds. "Congratulations. I'm sure you'll both be happy." She was joined by Belinda, "Forgive the others. A bunch of old fogies." Tommy and Adele took sips of the wine and no doubt the euphoria of wedded bliss dulled their palate for it increased their smiles.

"So tell me," said Hazel, "what brought on this happy event?"

"We'd been hiking in the Grampians and had a call from the police to return after the murder of Jake. We had to explain our movements, but we were miles away camping, so there was nothing to tell really," said Tommy.

"And we didn't know him at all,' said Adele, in a small voice. "We both recently turned twenty, so decided to marry and had set up the arrangement with the registry office. We've just come from there."

"What about your parents? Your family? Were they there?" said Belinda.

"Neither of us have a family. We met at socially and..."

"And one thing led to another," said Belinda with a smile. 'Nice to hear a happy story after all the bad news,"

"It was while we were at the police station that we heard of Max's funeral and hurried over. We didn't want to miss it."

"How did you meet Max?" asked Belinda.

The newlyweds exchanged a glance. "Well, we belong to a few film society groups, and somewhere along the line, Max was mentioned, and we tracked him down," said Tommy.

"We were keen to hear about film in the old days, you know, way back before our time,' added Adele condescendingly. Hazel, hackles rising, was about to comment when Belinda, anticipating her sharp reply, said, "And did he tell you?"

Tommy smiled a secret smile. "Yes. Some very interesting things."

'Like what' thought Hazel?

Leaving Hazel to discover this, Belinda excused herself and made her way over to Muriel. "Can you tell me where the bathroom is?" Muriel nodded. "There's one along the hall. At the end. I don't know what condition it's in. There is another upstairs just down from Max's bedroom, which is probably better."

Belinda smiled her thanks and made her way to the entrance hall. Once there she hurried up the staircase. It seemed logical the VHS tapes would be in the room Max was murdered in. It was a Pandora's Box of films, film equipment, magazines, and photos. Of course, they might be in any room in this rambling house, but it seemed wise to start with the obvious location. The police security lock had been removed, and Belinda stepped gingerly into the musty room. Blood stains on the wooden floor brought back the horror of Max's death, and she hurried across to several shelves bursting with film cans. A swift inspection revealed no videotapes. Towards the rear of the room was a large built-in annex that again was crammed with film paraphernalia. It was dark, and Belinda fumbled for a light switch. As she did so, the sound of approaching footsteps made her freeze. To explain what she was doing there would be difficult so she melted back into the shadows hoping she wouldn't be discovered. The footsteps sounded louder and finally stopped at the door. A pause, and they continued across the room to the annex. A hand switched on the light and Belinda was revealed. She looked up at the intruder. It was Lance.

"I saw you leave the group and wondered why, and what you were up to?"

Belinda edged away. "I was looking for the bathroom."

"Well as you can see, this is not it," said Lance gruffly. The stark overhead light cast deep shadows on his face creating a deathlike mask. His hand on the light switch was large and powerful. He edged closer to her. "We're getting tired of you and your pommy friend sticking your nose into our business. What do these murders have to do with you?"

Belinda raised her chin defiantly. "As we've said before, we accidentally got involved and treated like suspects, and we just want to see a resolution."

Lance's hand poked Belinda on the shoulder. "The resolution might not be the one you think it to be. The last time we spoke you practically accused me of being the murderer."

"No, I suggested you were among the suspects, as we all are."

"Not how I took it. And I don't appreciate a stranger coming into my group. Until you arrived, it was a happy group of people all with a similar background."

Belinda thought he was being delusional or

defensive. "A happy group prepared to tie an old man up and keep him prisoner so they could get a valuable film from him after he refused to sell it?"

Belinda felt threatened as Lance moved closer until he was almost face to face with her. Again the jab on the shoulder. This time much harder. "Just mind your own business from now on," he snarled, "or you might find yourself joining Max and the boy." He turned and strode out of the room. Belinda breathed a sigh of relief and rubbed her sore shoulder. She was surprised at his anger; he'd seemed a gentle soul, so what was it that brought on this violent change? She didn't believe his threat but was intrigued to know what was behind it. Peer pressure from the others in the group? Had he been elected to lean on this interloper?

As she watched him leave she saw, packed away on a shelf, a small suitcase. Pulling it out and brushing the dust away, she opened it. The contents were a higgledy-piggledy collection of commercial VHS tapes of various old films, their colourful covers depicting a long-forgotten publicity department's idea of the contents, along with several famous German silent films. She glanced at their titles and the names of their famous directors. At the bottom of the case, two tapes were labelled merely, TAPE 2. TAPE 5. These *had* to be the tapes she was looking for. Putting them aside she replaced the suitcase and made her way to the staircase. Hiding the tapes as best she could in her snug jacket, she returned to the ground floor. At the foot of the stairs stood

Muriel. "Did you find what you were looking for?" Was it Belinda's imagination? What was the woman implying?

Belinda smiled. "Yes. Eventually. I stopped to look at some of the fittings in other rooms. I love this late Victorian period."

"Yes," said Muriel, "there's a lot to interest one. If you know where to look."

Again Belinda thought this ambiguous comment was an indication that Muriel was suspicious. She went to the Garden Room where Hazel had Sam bailed up against the wall lecturing him on the failure of the European Commission.

Belinda nudged her. "Mission accomplished."

Hazel gave a nod, spat one last expletive-ridden comment on the EC, and took Belinda's arm. This dislodged one of the VHS tapes, TAPE 5 clattered to the stone floor. All eyes were on it. Belinda hurriedly picked it up. "Just catching up on the silent films of F W Murnau, but I expect you know who he is anyway."

The group was as silent as Murnau's films, but their eyes followed the two women as they made their escape. Hazel whispered. "Who the hell is F W Murnau?"

Belinda clutched the tapes close to her. "You tell me. I just saw his name on a video cover."

Chapter Eleven

"Oh, he's just full of piss and wind." Hazel reaction to Belinda's story of harassment by Lance was to dismiss it. "After all, what can he do to you?"

"Well for one thing, he could murder me," replied Belinda acerbically. "Let's not forget he is still a suspect, and if he bumped off Max and Jake, I doubt he'd have any second thoughts before dispatching me." They had settled down with a pot of tea and some carnal cakes from an Italian bakery, to view Jake's VHS tapes of the interviews with Max.

"With only two tapes, we have no way of knowing how many were made and where the others are," said Belinda, licking a dollop of cream from her upper lip.

"Jake said ten, I think. So we'll just have to hope that there's something of interest in these two." She pressed the start button, and the machine whirred into action. The screen flashed on and off and on again, wavered through a lot of static and eventually settled on a man sitting in what they recognised to be the dining room in Max's house. The harsh black and white image gave the impression of earlier times with hard lighting adding a touch of German Expressionism. Whether this was intentional by Jake or by chance, but it certainly added a layer of drama to the interview.

Now, at last, they had a good look at Max. His face had been so battered when he was murdered they had no clear idea of his appearance. What they saw was a chubby elderly man seated in a high-backed grandfather chair. By his side a small table with a bottle of port from which, frequently, he refreshed his glass. He was dressed rather flamboyantly in a smoking jacket with a silk scarf draped around his neck. What little grey hair he retained was combed over a bald pate in parallel lines like regimented Ley Lines, those mysterious lines that run between monuments and ancient archaeological sites, or in this case, his ears. His face was round, surprisingly free from wrinkles, heavy dark eyebrows dominated suspicious eyes, and several chins supported the whole.

The anomaly was his voice. High pitched with a slight lisp, it was excited, energetic, and pompous. It was also delicately slurred indicating he had consumed a reasonable quantity of port previous to the recording. Between constant refilling's of his glass and chain-smoking, he regaled the camera with tales of his father and his expertise as a cinematic showman by running a number of small art cinemas that relied on European films, thereby creating a following of cinéastes who abhorred Hollywood melodramas. The old man, Jean de Lautour had come from France at the end of World War Two, where he'd been a projectionist in the Studio des Ursulines in the 5th Arrondissement screening avant-garde treats to the French intelligentsia of the day. With his contacts in Europe, he would purchase one copy of a film and screen it until it fell to pieces, but making a comfortable living from each one. He was amused to screen François Truffaut's Jules et Jim part of which took place in the Studio des Ursulines, and he took advantage of this to promote himself and the film, by giving press interviews and detailing his time at that Parisian cinematic temple.

His own cinemas were small, often in run-down buildings where the rent was cheap. The staff consisted of a girl in the box office selling tickets and sweets at the interval. As projectionists, for little money, he employed young men, often students, who were film struck and the opportunity to actually handle film was the elixir of life. Seating was hard and uncomfortable, 'one must suffer for Art' and the premises dark and dusty. And so this was Max's introduction to film and its mysteries.

The tape lasted half an hour by which time Belinda and Hazel had consumed the tea and cakes, and felt bloated not only in body but in mind by Max's twittering's which were often interrupted by a roar of laughter as he detailed his early life. With some relief, Hazel ejected the tape and inserted the second one. She sank back into her chair. "Well that's thirty minutes I'll never get back. Let's hope this tape gives us something of value."

The second cassette TAPE 5 was recorded on another day as witnessed by the location which had Max sitting up in bed, a plethora of papers and magazines scattered around him, and empty wine bottles. He was very drunk, waved a glass of wine around to emphasise his remarks, and regaled the camera with how his father had bought an even smaller cinema than the ones he owned and put Max in charge of it. It was Max's chance to screen the type of films he preferred which were B grade blood and guts, horror tales that he acquired as cheaply as possible. In a moment of reflection, he recalled the difference in tastes between his father and himself. The old man preferred art films and sought out cinematic gems to screen. One, in particular, was an early Australian film.

Both Belinda and Hazel were suddenly alert.

MAX: Something to do with some religious group... the Sallies, that's it. Salvation Army. Seems they put on a show with slides and bits of film...

JAKE (off-screen): When was that?

MAX: ...who knows? Who cares? But before any other films were made. Silly old fart paid a fortune for the negs.

(He paused and looked bewildered) They're here somewhere...don't remember where...

JAKE: Could I see them?

MAX: If you can find them. Probably not much good now.

JAKE: Still, they could be worth something.

MAX: Better to find the print.

JAKE: What print?

MAX: 'Old man had a print made from the neg. Got some bloke who ran a film lab in Collingwood to run off a print. A copy.

JAKE: Do you have the print?

MAX: Do I? Can't remember. Probably yes. Probably

no.

(He gestured dismissively, spilling wine on the bed. He became distracted in mopping it up)

JAKE: This dude who made the copy? Is he still alive? What was his name?

MAX: How do you expect me to remember... wait on...Bert something or other... funny old bloke...

(He drained the last of the wine from his glass and peered at an empty bottle)

JAKE: When did this happen?

MAX: Oh, about thirty ...forty years ago... long time ago...Bert Ballard...that's the bloke's name. Just remembered...

JAKE: And you don't know where the print is?

MAX: Who cares? (He sniggered) I'll tell you a funny story about a bloke arrested for indecent behaviour in my cinema. We were running a soft porn movie, and there were a lot of pervs in the audience. Seems he said he was looking for a friend. Elsie who ran the candy bar said, 'If you ask me, they're all looking for a friend.' Now, be a good lad and run down to the kitchen, and bring up another bottle of red...

He waved an empty bottle at the camera and the image froze for a second and the screen went black. There was nothing else on the tape.

Both women sat in silence for a moment as they absorbed what they had heard. Hazel broke the silence with a plea. "I need a drink." Putting actions to the words she rose and poured a gin and tonic. One good gulp allowed her to put her thoughts into words. "So, there is a copy of the missing film. Point is, do the others in the group know about it? And if they do, what are they going to do?"

Belinda scratched her nose. "My guess is they don't know but realise that Jake was in the house the night of the murder looking for something. They saw the tape I dropped and putting two and two together might assume that *it* was what he was searching for. They knew I was looking for something, Lance's appearance and threats prove that. As for what they're going to do, we'll have to wait and see."

***

Across town, the group reassembled in the Garden Room. After the departure of Belinda and Hazel they had been galvanised into action and, as one, rushed upstairs to thoroughly search Max's rooms, uncertain of what they were looking for, but on the evidence of the tape Belinda dropped, a thorough search was made for, and of, any videotape they could locate. Disappointed they returned empty-handed to contemplate what their next course of action should be. If Belinda had something relating to the historic film, they wanted it. After much discussion, some members left, with only Harry, Charmaine, Lance, and Bridie remaining.

"That woman wouldn't have taken the tape on a whim. She knows something, and we need to know what it is," said Harry.

Lance turned to Bridie. "You know where

she lives. Give me her address."

Bridie smiled at the thought of betraying her old school chum, the high and mighty Ms. Lawrence with her inheritance and silver spoon in her mouth. "Yes. It's East Melbourne. I'll write it down for you." She proceeded to write on a paper serviette from the table.

"What are you going to do?" asked Harry.

"I think to pay her a visit. I warned her off earlier on. This time I'll be more persuasive."

***

"How are we going to track down this Bert Ballard," said Hazel. It was the next morning, and she was brewing coffee. "And does that film lab still exist?"

"The logical person to ask is Bridie, but if we do that she will want to know why, and that will get back to the others in the group. And I don't want Lance making any more threats on me," said Belinda.

Hazel poured two cups of coffee. "Who knows if Bert Ballard is still alive? It all happened a long time ago."

"We can Google the film lab and see if it still operates, although I doubt it, what with everything going digital, and also search online for Bert."

"I've just had a thought," said Hazel, "why not try asking Joe O'Brien? He's old enough to remember those times and probably knew of the lab and maybe even knew Bert. And I doubt if he'd mention it to anyone in the group, he's so vague."

"Good idea. Do we know where he and Muriel live?"

"I can look up the phone directory, my guess is they have a landline phone," said Hazel. "While you talk to Joe, it will give me a chance to grill Muriel and see what she knows, and also ask her to go over what happened on the night Max was murdered."

Belinda took her coffee and wandered into the living room. The two videotapes remained where she's left them the previous day. Out in the open. Vulnerable. Given the information contained within, perhaps they should be made safe. She cast an eye over a collection of DVD's and CD's along the wall.

***

Lance drove slowly down the East Melbourne Street searching for Belinda's house. He came across the number he was looking for and pulled his car into the gutter to park. The street was quiet with no other traffic. Belinda's house was an Edwardian red brick building sandwiched in between late Victorian terraces, monuments from the gold rush days. Nearby a woman swept the path to her garden and then disappeared inside. He had no real plan on what he wanted to do and was prepared to wait until he saw any signs of life at Belinda's house. He didn't have to wait long. Crouching down to conceal his presence he watched as Belinda and Hazel crossed the rose garden in front of the house. They were in conversation and paid no heed to any nearby activities but got into a car and drove off.

Lance stepped out of his car and crossed the road. He paused at the garden gate with no way of knowing if anyone else was home. If so, how would he handle it? Pretend to be a salesman? Looking for directions? No. Better to be up front and say he was from a group that Belinda knew of, and he wanted to speak to her. About some videotapes. The woman next door appeared again and tipped a bucket of water into the gutter. She noticed him standing at Belinda's gate and stood to watch him. Aware of the woman, Lance turned to her and smiled. "I was just admiring these autumn roses." The woman made no reply but eventually gave a nod of acceptance and returned inside closing the door behind her.

Lance waited. There was no one else in the street. Cautiously he opened the gate and stepped into the garden. The perfume from the roses held sway. Stepping up to the porch he pushed the bell, heard it echoing inside. No immediate response, so he rang again. Still no answer. Taking a chance that the house was empty, he walked along the side of the house, opened a wooden gate and continued on to the back.

Several small windows offered themselves as potential entry points. One window has a crack in the bottom of the glass. Looking around, Lance selected a medium sized rock from a small ornamental garden display. He pulled a tea towel from a nearby bush where it had been left to dry. Wrapping the towel around his hand, he took hold of the rock, grimaced, and smashed the glass. Weakened by the crack the window shattered and glass fragments fell noisily to the concrete path.

Holding his breath, he waited in silence for any reaction. But there was none. He was able to reach in and release the simply latch. The window swung open on its hinges. With ease, he was able to lift himself up and climb through the window. He was in a small larder off the kitchen. It occurred to him that if he was discovered, he might need some form of defence. He still didn't know if there was anyone in the house and it was possible that Belinda and Hazel would return at any minute. Glancing around, he saw some kitchen utensils. Including a large knife. He grasped it and gingerly began his progress into the kitchen. He had no idea where the videotape would be, and it might take some time to search this large house but working on the assumption the tapes would be near a video player, and that player was usually in the lounge or sitting room, he began his quest. The knife held firmly before him he entered the hallway and edged past several rooms until he was at the front of the house. On his left was the place he was looking for, the living room, where he was likely to find the videotapes. The shades were drawn rendering the room gloomy, but he could make out chairs and a settee before an open fireplace. Nearby, a TV set and a DVD player as well as an old VHS machine. On a coffee table beneath he saw the tapes TAPE 2. TAPE 5.

He was about to pick them up when a nearby phone rang, its metallic reverberation sounding exceptionally loud in the silent house. Lance held his breath waiting for the ringing to stop. But it went on and on. Cautiously he picked up the handset.

"Belinda? Is that you…I've tried ringing on your mobile but it's switched off, so I tried your parent's number…Belinda? …are you there?"

Lance quietly replaced the receiver. He knew that voice. It belonged to Bridie Kelly. Why was she calling Belinda? Was she ringing to warn her he had her address? And if so, why? Double-dealing? With these thoughts in his head, he picked up the tapes. At least he could see what Belinda prized in them. One final act, driven by anger. He plunged the knife into the coffee table. It stood erect as an ominous warning to Ms. Belinda Lawrence – keep out of the Group's business!

Chapter Twelve

The tantalizing aroma of home cooking wafted towards Belinda and Hazel as Muriel opened the door in answer to their knock.

"Hello, Muriel," said Belinda, "I rang before, asking if we could chat with Joe. Thanks for agreeing to meet with us."

Muriel wiped her hands on a worn butcher's apron that strained across her bulky figure. She smiled. "You're welcome I'm sure. Joe likes nothing better than to talk about the old days. Come in." She led then down the hall of the bungalow to the lounge where Joe was dozing before a TV, where Esther Williams was about to plunge from a great height to what looked like her inevitable death.

"Joe, dear. Wake up. You have visitors." She switched off the TV. Joe stirred. He'd been dreaming of screening a film in some vast unknown cinema, and Bette Davis and Joan Crawford came down from the screen and invited him to afternoon tea. Joan slipped a pill into Bette's tea, and Bette reciprocated by lacing Joan's cake with rat poison. They were both about to consume the deadly comestibles when Muriel's voice sounded from the cinema loudspeakers. He muttered, opened his eyes and saw the two young women who had been with the group the day Max was murdered. What did they want with him?

His answer came from Muriel. "Darl, these

two young ladies want to ask you about your life and films that you've seen. Sit up, and I'll make a pot of tea. I've just made some pumpkin scones so I'll go and prepare them now."

"May I help you?" said Hazel, as she quickly followed Muriel to the kitchen. Left alone with Joe, Belinda sat beside him on an armchair. He looked at her through watery eyes.

"Mister O'Brien, may I call you Joe?"

Joe nodded. "What do you want to know? If it's anything about how old Max died I…

"Oh no," said Belinda quickly. It's just that you've had such a long career in the film business and I'd like to hear some of your adventures.

Joe relaxed and smiled. He liked nothing better than talking about the past. Not much sense in talking about the future. "You're very kind to take an interest in an old bloke like me. Where do you want me to start?" Without waiting for a reply he began a tale of how, as a child, he'd been taken to see his first film. It was a Charlie Chaplin but he couldn't remember the title, all he could remember was…

Belinda began to worry that his rambling would take all day. "I suppose you didn't screen any Australian films?"

Joe looked bewildered. "Australian films? No. No, there weren't any. Chipps Rafferty had a go, made a couple. And Charles Cheval, but no."

"I heard there was a small film laboratory in Collingwood, do you remember it?"

"Collingwood? I know there was one in East Melbourne, but..."

"I believe a man by the name of Bert Ballard worked there."

Joe looked thoughtful. "It was a small town in those days and anybody in the film biz knew everyone else." He turned to a small chest of drawers. "Have a look in the bottom drawer. I think I have an old phone address book somewhere."

Belinda opened the draw. An abundance of memorabilia lay before her. "It has a black cover with a signed picture of Ann Miller on it. I stuck it on when she was in Melbourne to promote a film. 'Got to meet her. Lovely lady," said Joe.

Belinda rummaged through the keepsakes of the old projectionist. Eventually Ann Miller peeped out from under Clark Gable. She took the frail book and handed to Joe. He made himself comfortable and began searching. "What did you say his name was?" One name made him smile. "Oh, dear old Maisie. She sold candy at the Regent. I suppose she's dead by now."

Fearing Joe would get lost in a wave of nostalgia she sat near him. "Bert Ballard is the name we're looking for. Search under 'B.'"

It took a moment for Joe to respond as he found several other names from the past that brought back memories as well as reminding him they were probably no longer of this world. "Ballard, you say? Let's see." He flicked back pages until he found what he wanted; his finger ran down the names. Muttering to himself he read them. "Baker. Betty C. Bondi. Ballard! Strike me pink. There he is, Bert Ballard from Kinematone Labs, and yes the address was in Collingwood."

"Great," said Belinda, "do you know what became of him?"

Joe searched the ceiling. "Struth, that's a long time ago. Wait… I think I heard he was in a nursing home. He must be about ninety by now, that is if he hasn't carked it."

"Do you know the name of the nursing home?"

Joe shook his head. "No. As I said it was a long time ago and we were never really close friends. But…I seem to remember it was somewhere down the bay, Mornington or Portsea. On the peninsula. A lot of people retire down that way."

***

In the kitchen Muriel filled the kettle and placed it on the stove. Lighting the gas she said, "Joe likes to talk about the old days. I hope he isn't boring Belinda too much."

"I'm sure she will enjoy it," said Hazel. She watched as Muriel began to butter the scones. "Tell me, Muriel. What alibi did you give the police for the day Max was murdered?"

Muriel paused in what she was doing. "No worries dear, but I don't see why I should tell you. But if you must know, after I dropped off the cake

I went to my part-time job. I clean other people's houses. The pension doesn't go far these days." Her broad shoulders rigid in a line of defence, she resumed buttering,

Shamefaced, Hazel said, "Can I do anything to help?"

Muriel spoke over her shoulder. "That would be nice, can you get the cups and saucers from out the cupboard. It's the one at the bottom."

Hazel turned to the cupboard near her. There were two doors. Making a guess she opened one and a number of metal objects fell to the floor. Muriel turned sharply. "No. Not that one, the other. That one is Joe's film bits and pieces, rewinds and things."

Hazel began to replace the items. "I know what this is. I've seen one before. It's for rewinding films. Awkward heavy things."

Muriel dropped the scones and hurried over. "I keep telling Joe he'll have to get rid of all that rubbish." She took the cumbersome object by the handle and hurriedly replaced it in the cupboard. Shutting the door firmly, she returned to the scones. Hazel began to remove the cups and saucers from the other cupboard. "I can see why he'd like to hang on to mementoes from his past."

Muriel put tea leaves into the pot. "They can be a temptation. Better to get rid of them. Sometimes they bring back bitter memories."

"Talking of memories," said Hazel, "Max's death must have stirred up some?"

"For Joe and the group member's maybe, but I wasn't really part of it. I only went for Joe's sake. He did so look forward to the screenings."

"You must have gathered an opinion about the members?!

Muriel poured some milk into a jug. "Oh yes, I think I had them all figured out. Harry was a bully, no doubt about that. Bridie is a flibbertigibbet, at least that's what we called her type in my day."

"An airhead? said Hazel.

Muriel thought for a moment. "Yes, I suppose that's about right but I prefer flibbertigibbet. Lance is a bit of a mystery man to me. Seems as though he's keeping a secret. The two young ones? Who can tell? They seem likable, if a bit colourless. I had very little to do with them. Although thinking about it, it seemed odd how they just suddenly appeared and were accepted into the group. Sam?" Muriel paused, "Sam – I'd rather not say."

"Which brings us to Charmaine," said Hazel.

Muriel gave her a sly glance. "I don't have to tell you about Charmaine. You've got her figured out already, I can tell."

Hazel smiled and nodded. Muriel poured the boiling water into the teapot. "I will say this about her, she was looking for bread to butter but on both sides. It was a tossup between Harry and Max. My guess she preferred Max to marry, then she would inherit any money he had and the house. She'd be set for her old age." She paused in what she was doing and turned to Hazel, a look of concern on her face. "I'm glad I've got the chance to talk to you. I need some advice. You see, I rather told a lie to the police about the day Max was murdered. Told them I dropped in to deliver the cake, which was true, but I also told them I didn't see anyone else at the house."

"What did you see," said Hazel, eager now to hear what the woman would reveal.

"Well, I suppose I'll have to tell the police and they won't like it, saying I was withholding evidence or whatever. And they can charge me with that, can't they? I hope not. What will happen to Joe? Anyway, what I didn't tell them is... that I did see someone else at the house that afternoon."

"Who?" Hazel almost shrieked at the prospect of hearing this bombshell.

"Well, I put the sponge in the fridge and looked out the window and saw them going into the house. It was Harry and Lance."

There was a moment's silence as the two women looked at each other. Muriel with a bland expression; Hazel with wide-eyed wonder. "Now," said Muriel, as though she'd just casually revealed her secret recipe for pumpkin scones, "tea's made. Let's see if Joe has run out of steam."

Each taking a tray loaded with scones and tea, Hazel barely able to walk in a straight line due to shock, they joined Joe and Belinda. As they entered the room they heard Belinda a say, "Thanks for telling me about him."

Tea was served, scones consumed amid

complements on Muriel's cooking, and a tsunami of memories from Joe including the peak of his career working at the Metro Collins Street and screening the pick of MGM films. Hazel hardly ate a thing and was fidgeting, eager to get away and tell Belinda her news. Eventually Joe grew hoarse and Belinda and Hazel made their excuses, with lavish thanks to their hosts. Muriel saw them to the door, and waved goodbye. Hazel practically ran to their car, so eager was she to tell Belinda what Muriel had revealed. Watching them leave, Muriel had to push the door hard for the lock to catch and made another mental note to have it fixed otherwise an intruder need only give the door a good shove to gain entry. She made her way slowly, thoughtfully, down the hall. Joe was about to put in another videotape from his collection. Muriel put her hand on his to stop him. He looked up at her. "What did you tell Belinda," she asked bitingly.

***

The tyres swerved onto the footpath knocking over a garbage bin, before Belinda swung the steering wheel and got the car back on the road.

"She said *what*?" Hazel had just revealed everything Muriel had told her in the kitchen and it came as such a surprise that for a moment she lost control of the motor. "Both Harry and Lance? Has she told the police?"

Hazel shook her head. "She says she hasn't

and is worried about withholding evidence."

Belinda glanced at her. "You realise if she doesn't, you'll have to tell the police what she said."

Hazel fidgeted uncomfortably with her seat belt. "Well...let's see if she does. I don't want to get more involved than I am with the boys in blue." They drove on and were still discussing Muriel's claim when they arrived back at Belinda's house. Belinda went to check her emails and Hazel headed for the drinks cabinet. The living room was getting dark as the afternoon light began to fade and she switched on a table lamp. She took a glass and tipped in a generous serve of gin, and was just reaching for the tonic when she gave a shriek of horror. The gin and the tonic were wasted on the carpet.

Lit now by the lamp, the gleaming ugly blade of a carving knife, impaled in the coffee table, sent a shiver up her spine.

***

Lance fumbled in his eagerness to view the tapes he'd found at Belinda's house and, confident that they contained something of importance to the group, sat nervously through TAPE 2. His two cats sat assiduously beneath the screen seemingly absorbed in Max's ramblings. It was disappointing as it contained nothing but the rabbiting on of Old Max in his cups as usual, and he was tempted to high speed through, but was reluctant to in case he missed something of value. His mind wandered and he again thought of Bridie and her mysterious phone call to Belinda. He'd have to get to the bottom of that.

The tape eventually ended and he replaced it with TAPE 5. He sat back, took a sip of his vodka, and hoped for the best. It seemed to be more of the same; he was beginning to think he was on a wild goose chase, but there had to be something about the tapes, otherwise why would that girl steal it? He was just about the admit failure when a remark made by Jake made him sit up.

JAKE: Do you have the print?

MAX: Do I? Can't remember. Probably yes. Probably no.

(He gestured dismissively, spilling wine on the bed. He became distracted in mopping it up)

JAKE: This dude who made the copy? Is he still alive? What was his name?

MAX: How do you expect me to remember... wait on...Bert something or other... funny old bloke...

(He drained the last of the wine from his glass and peered at an empty bottle)

JAKE: When did this happen?

MAX: Oh, about thirty ...forty years ago... long time ago...Bert...

...

The screen suddenly went blank then filled with ecstatic revellers in drag wearing more feathers than a franchise of ostriches – and little else. Lance gave a cry of anger and threw his glass at the TV. It missed but hit the cats, who screamed at him in rage and ran for cover under a table.

There was a thunderous knocking at his front door. The cats cowered even further under the table. Lance glanced out the side window and he could see other retired residents standing in groups, all chattering and all watching his cottage. He edged quietly to the door. One look through the security peephole told him why the neighbours were so captivated. A scandal on their very own doorsteps. It was the police.

***

Belinda struggled to remove the knife from the table. It had been driven in with such force its removal took some effort. At last it was freed and she exchanged it with Hazel for a glass of wine. Hazel with some distaste hurriedly put the knife on the drinks cabinet.

"I need this," said Belinda, as she took a sip of wine. "Whoever it was, broke in through a window at the back. I've been at mum and dad to make the house more secure, what with all the break-ins we hear of."

Hazel eyed the gin bottle at her elbow. "This 'whoever' you mention. It must have been one of the group. The videotapes are gone, and nothing else seems to be missing."

"Yes. And from the group it has to be either Harry or Lance, and my money is on the latter."

Hazel, silently fretting over the wasted gin,

and still evaluating on a scale of one to ten the level of shock she had received, settled on nine. This she felt was severe enough to warrant consolation. The aromatic restorative flowed into her glass. "Possibly, after he threatened you at Max's house. But if he has the tape, he will know about the old boke, Bert and the copy of the film," said Hazel.

Belinda's eyes sparkled above the rim of her glass. "I can guarantee he won't. I took the trouble to copy the tapes to a DVD and wiped part of the tape, so the information about Bert has gone. I taped over it with the gay Mardi Grass from Sydney.

Hazel raised her glass. "Not just a pretty face. How clever. I'd love to be a fly in the wall when he realises the most important part of the tape is missing and he's stuck watching drag queens. Where is the DVD? Will they come looking for that?"

"Assuming they get to hear about it, which I doubt, I've buried in among my dad's CD collection of Viennese Waltzes, which is a bit like hiding it in a cursed tomb. No one dares approach it."

Chapter Thirteen

Muriel's statement to the police that she had seen both Harry and Lance enter the house on the day of Max's murder saw the entire group including Belinda and Hazel, being interviewed again at police headquarters. Hazel confirmed that Muriel had told her she witnessed the two men at the house and signed an affidavit to this effect. Both Harry and Lance strongly denied the accusation confirming their original statements after they were told an unnamed witness had made a declaration to police.

"So it's hearsay, and we're the only ones who know who made the accusation," said Belinda, as they left headquarters, "Muriel's word against theirs."

"And who is telling the truth?" said Hazel.

"Muriel, Lance, and Sam admit being there, but what of Harry and Charmaine?"

"Apparently Charmaine says she was shopping but also claims to have been with Harry, but there is no proof she was," said Hazel, "and so far we have no idea what Harry was doing, even though Lance claims to have seen his car in the street."

"Both of them could have hidden in the house earlier, and no one would have been the wiser," said Belinda. They mulled over these possibilities on the tram back to East Melbourne. Once home, Belinda headed for the computer. "We can speculate on who murdered Max until the cows come home, but right now, I want to locate nursing homes down on the peninsula."

***

The sea air on the drive from Melbourne to the Mornington peninsula dispersed the city smog and grime, and both Belinda and Hazel felt invigorated and energised. With Hazel driving, Belinda gave her attention to the radio and the tenor singing a Rossini aria. The melody introduced a sentimental mood, and her thoughts turned to Mark Sallinger, her one-time lover. The breakup had been painful as she realised Mark would never really settle down, and for all his wealth his craving to increase his fortune dominated his life and had they married, Belinda knew she would have spent many lonely days and nights as Mark jetted from one side of the word to the other, planting and tilling his financial pastures. This was not the life she planned or wanted. With a sigh, she consigned Mark to his golden asylum which she felt he was predestined to inhabit. A wrong choice. Now she could admit it.

Other thoughts filtered in among those of a disenchanted love affair.

Thoughts more profane.

Max's pulverized face. The bruises on his body. The ropes binding him.

And the group. All had keys to the house. Most of them were at the house at some time of the day of the murder.

After Muriel's accusations that Harry and Lance were seen to enter the house, how did their alibis stand up now?

Harry and Charmaine had not really given any reliable evidence of their activities on the day of the murder.

And what of Muriel? Was she telling the truth?

All this over a piece of film that now didn't exist – unless there was a copy and only Bert Ballard could supply that information. If he was capable of doing so. The nurse she had spoken to at the nursing home, didn't hold much hope and indicated that Bert spent his time in bed and was mostly asleep.

It had taken many phone calls to find the nursing home, and Belinda used the excuse that she was a distant relative of Bert's and only discovered his whereabouts and wanted to meet him before he... well, while he was still with us. The vista of the bay spread out before them as they motored into Sorrento where the home was located, right on the end of the peninsula. Set in gardens, it was a mansion that had once been the home of a millionaire, but now provided comfort to souls, as they hemmed and hawed awaiting an imprecise divine decree.

"You're lucky," said the nurse as she led Belinda and Hazel down a brightly lit corridor, "Bert's quite calm today. Had his lunch without throwing the tapioca pudding at Nurse Nguyet."

Bert's room faced a garden with French windows leading out. They were open, and the ocean spices wafted in relieving the room of any Judgement Day ambience. Bert sat up in bed, sheets covering him up to his shoulders. Only his bald head was visible, but it had bright eyes peering at them through old-fashioned round spectacles. Belinda was reminded of Mahatma Gandhi in his last days.

A beaming smile and a thin piping voice greeted them. "Are you from the spindle side or the spear side of the family?"

Belinda smiled. "Neither, Mister Ballard. We know some friends of yours. Friends who worked in the cinema, projectionists and usherettes. My name's Belinda, and this is Hazel."

Bert looked smug. "I'm ninety-three. In six years I'll be one hundred."

Belinda, who didn't bother to correct his mathematical miscalculation, wondered if his mind was beginning to wander. "Congratulations, Bert. May I call you Bert?"

"That's my name," said Bert, lucidly, "so I don't know what else you could call me."

Hazel, who was beginning to feel uncomfortable in surroundings that hinted at the presence of the Grim Reaper, thought it was time to cut to the chase. "Bert, do you remember a man called Jean de Lautor? He had a son named Max."

Bert's eyes swivelled towards Hazel, appraising eyes that had seen a lot, eyes that were now making judgement. "Why would an attractive young woman like you, ask such a question?"

Hazel preened at the compliment, even if it

came from a bedridden geriatric.

"Lulu," continued Bert, "With that hairstyle, you remind me of her. Louise Brooks, the silent film star. She was a looker too. Pity she's dead."

Hazel, reminded of her mortality, demanded hoarsely, "But you do remember him?"

Bert turned his attention back to Belinda. "Can you explain why she wants to know?"

Belinda smiled and sent a censorious glance to Hazel. "You must forgive her. She can be over enthusiastic at times. But we do want to know if you recall Jean de Lautor from the days when you had the film laboratory in Melbourne."

The old man looked piqued. "Yes. I remember him. And his son, Max. Is the son still alive?"

"No. He died," said Belinda.

"Oh good," said Bert with a contented smile, "that's another one I've beaten. How did he die?"

"He was murdered."

Bert considered this and gave a nod of approval. "Yes, I can see why he would be."

Again, Hazel feeling they were drifting, stepped closer to the bed. "The point is did this de Lautor fellow get you to make a print of an old film that he had the negatives for?"

Bert looked up as she towered over him. "Forty-six pounds and ten shillings."

Hazel and Belinda both frowned. "What do you mean?" asked Belinda.

"That's what he owes me. He never paid me for the sixteen-millimetre copy I made for him, from some old silent film footage he'd found. He took the negative back but refused to pay for the print. Said it was highway robbery, so I kept the print."

"And do you still have it?" said Belinda and Hazel in unison.

Bert glanced around the sterile room. "I don't have anything now. All gone. But it's best this way."

"Do you know what happened to the film?" said Belinda.

Bert looked thoughtful. "Don't know. It could have ended up with my sister. Most of my belongings went to her." He yawned widely.

Hazel, fearing he would nod off said, "If we find it we can pay you for it."

This brought Bert back from the arms of Morpheus with some alacrity. "All forty-six pounds and ten shillings?"

"With ten percent interest," said Belinda.

Bert did a mental calculation. "Alright. My sister's name is Daisy Ballard. She never married. When you see her, you'll know why."

"Do you have her address," said Hazel.

There was a silence as Bert rummaged through his mental debris and slowly shook his head. "No. Somewhere in Melbourne. That's all I can remember at the moment."

Belinda took a notepad and from her bag and wrote on it. "Bert, if you do remember, can you call Hazel or me, or get one of the nurses to call us on these numbers?" She placed the note on the bedside cabinet. Bert gave a sleepy nod, and he sank back into the pillow as the thought of forty-six pounds and ten shillings, plus ten percent interest, comforted him as he returned to his appointment with Morpheus.

As they entered the foyer, Belinda went to the reception desk. "Excuse me, we've just been visiting Mister Ballard, and he mentioned a sister. I was wondering if you could give me her address."

The receptionist looked bewildered. "A sister? That's news to me. He came here claiming he had no one in the world." She turned to her computer. "Just a minute and I'll check his record." Various images flashed on the screen and her fingers flittered over the keyboard. "No. As I thought. No relatives." She turned to the women with a woebegone expression. "Sad to be all alone in the world.

Chapter Fourteen

"It's for sale! Hazel's shriek shattered the late morning calm of East Melbourne. Perusing that relic of past times, the Sunday Paper, she had been comparing house prices in London and Melbourne and wasn't that surprised to see very little difference.

"What's for sale," asked Belinda, as she finished writing an email to her parents somewhere on the high seas.

"Max's house," said Hazel, her nose buried in the paper. Belinda joined her. "Show me."
Beneath a rather glamorised photo, details of the sale were on display. "Deceased estate," read Belinda, "once in a life time opportunity to develop or create a sumptuous family home. In the same family since Eighteen-eighty-five first time offered for sale." She went on to read details of the number of rooms, surrounding gardens and out houses and suggestions for a potential buyer to develop.

"It seems rather soon after Max's death to be selling, doesn't it?" said Hazel. "Surely probate hasn't been settled."

"Yes, it does seem odd but since there is no family, they may have decided to move things along," said Belinda, her eyes still on the paper.

"When is the auction?" said Hazel.

"Next Saturday morning."

"Do you want to go?"

"Yes, if only to see if the group members

show up and who is likely to be a potential buyer," said Belinda, as she folded the paper. "We know none of the group will be able to afford it, but they might know of the copy of the film, if whoever stole Max's tape showed it to them, and may suspect it is still in the house." She pointed at the paper. "It's to be sold as is, which means all the contents are still there."

"So they might do a deal with the new owner to get their hands on all the films and equipment," agreed Hazel.

"A wild goose chase for them as we know the copy went to Bert Ballard's sister, wherever she is."

The following week went uneventfully and on the Saturday morning, accompanied by colourful balloons bopping in the sharp air, the Auction This Day flags went up outside Max's house. Open a half hour before the auction it saw a steady trail of interested persons trek through the house, most only there as voyeurs to gape and criticise the contents and fantasise on how they would restore the mansion to its former glory. If they had the money. If. That was unlikely as the estimated sale price began at $1.5 million dollars and expected to go much higher. When Belinda and Hazel arrived there was about one hundred spectators. They wandered back to the cinema but it was locked and deserted. Inquisitive observers peered into dusty windows speculating on the contents of the locked building. Hazel nudged Belinda, "Look over there."

A dark shape was bent digging in a flower

bed. It was a woman wearing a white smock and black coat. To complete her ensemble she featured a flat black hat, set at a rakish angle. As they approached they realised it was Muriel. Startled at their appearance she dropped a trowel and closed a large carrier bag, carrying the logo of a famous Bourke Street department store.

"Oh, you surprised me."

"What on earth are you doing?" said Belinda.

Muriel gave a guilty smile. "I know it looks odd, but there were beautiful daffodils here last Spring, and I'm digging up some bulbs. A pity for them to go to waste and they will provide a happy memory for Joe."

"I suppose so," said Hazel, "a nice thought."

Muriel hesitated, turned away, picked up the trowel, and began to dig at the surface of the soil in a lacklustre way.

Belinda and Hazel looked amused. "Doing gardening wearing her best leather gloves," whispered Hazel, with a laugh. They headed back to the street, taking their place at the rear of the crowd.

"I can't see any other members of the group," said Hazel, "I thought they'd all be here."

"I can," said Belinda, as the dumpy figure of Sam sidled up to them.

"Making a bid?" said Belinda with a smile.

Sam shook his head. "Wish I could but it's out of my league." He looked soulfully at the house. "I'm going to miss the screenings. It was always a place to escape to, like the old Saturday matinee when you were a kid. Something other than school and squabbling parents." He gave them a sad smile.

"Do you think the group will continue to meet at another place," said Hazel.

Sam gave her a look that suggested she was certifiable. "What? With everyone a suspected murderer?"

Hazel bristled slightly but realised that her question was indeed ridiculous. "So, as all the films and equipment are still in the house, will you be aiming to buy some?"

Sam in philosophical mood shook his head and muttered enigmatically, "Another time, another place."

They watched as Muriel appeared and scurried away clutching her carrier bag close to her. Belinda decided to change the subject. "It's odd that the house is being sold before probate."

"Apparently the executor can sell, on the proviso the sale is subject to probate," said Sam. He was silent for a moment and then added under his breath. "I guess he got what he wanted."

"Who?" asked Hazel. But Sam ignored her.

"I suppose as there is no family –" but the words froze on Belinda's lips. Walking down the side of the house and in deep conversation with the estate agent was Tommy and Adele. "Good grief," said Hazel, "they don't think they're going to buy it, do they?"

Sam looked at the young couple. "Probably

just taking a last look around." But Belinda's interest was taken by their appearance. Adele now had a blonde, fashionable hair fabrication, wore a bright yellow dress with polka dots, strappy heels, and a white Panama with a broad black band. Tommy wore a grey Blazer suit jacket, slim casual pants, blue open necked shirt and white chinois. All new, thought Belinda and judging by the quality, expensive. And they exhibited a superb air of insouciance that previously had been lacking.

The sales agent began in ear-splitting voice by advising buyers that the house had a heritage listing and was suitable as magnificent family home; a boutique hotel; a reception venue; or division into apartments. Belinda heard little of this as she was watching Tommy and Adele who stood off to the side occasionally commenting to the other agent, so it was some surprise when she heard "SOLD" ring out loudly and the house had been sold for $3.75 million.

The crowd began to drift away and two suited business men approached the agent and all shook hands. The agent turned to Tommy and Adele and beckoned them to follow, as the new owners were ushered into their newly acquired property. Both Belinda and Hazel watched somewhat slacked jawed as the young couple, hand in hand, smiling and laughing, disappeared through the front door.

***

The autumn breeze carried the threat of winter as it whispered through the half-naked trees in the park. Belinda and Hazel sat side by side on a park bench, their eyes firmly fixed on the recently auctioned house. An estate agent slapped a SOLD sign across the auction board and gathered up the auction flags and balloons. With these optimistic signs designed to attract purse holders gone, what was revealed? A slightly down at heel Victorian House awaiting transformation into whatever castle in the air the new owner decreed. These activities barely registered with the women; their thoughts in unison, were computing the presence of Tommy and Adele at the auction and the astounding evidence that they were connected in some way with the sale.

"Are you thinking, what I'm thinking," said Belinda.

"I probably was," said Hazel, "but now I'm thinking of a gin and tonic.

Before Belinda could continue, a movement at the front door caught her attention. Tommy and Adele appeared with an agent. There were goodbye's said, hands shaken, smiles all round, and the blissful couple hurried excitedly further down the street to a Mercedes-Benz, sleek and black like a dormant panther, top down, promising luxury, excitement and thrills for its master. In this case it appeared to be Tommy, as he helped Adele to take her passenger seat, and he had just opened the driver's door, when Belinda, followed by Hazel reached the car.

"Tommy, I'm surprised to see you and Adele here. The only other member of the group to show was Sam. What did you think of the result? Quiet a windfall for Max's estate, isn't it?"

"Yes. Very satisfying," said Tommy, as he slid into the driver's seat.

"We can't help wondering why you were with the sales agents," said Hazel, leaning on the windscreen. Tommy's brow creased in annoyance and his smile dried up.

"There's a perfectly good reason. Although I don't see how it is any business of yours."

"Maybe not," said Belinda, "but indulge us. With the congratulations heaped on you by the agents, we could be forgiven for thinking you owned the house."

Tommy brushed an imaginary piece of lint for his jacket. "And you'd be correct in your thinking."

Hazel leaned closer. "You own it?"

"Well, in a manner of speaking. Max left it to me and so the result of the sale comes to me."

Belinda and Hazel looked stunned. "But – why," asked Belinda.

Tommy gave an irritated sigh. "The old man adopted me when I was eighteen. He didn't have any family and, I suppose, wanted to feel that he would leave someone to carry on his lineage. I'd been raised by several foster parents and it was through them that we met."

"And so you sold the house? So much for

honouring his lineage," said Hazel.

"I didn't want the house and you don't need material things to carry on a legacy. Besides, the executor suggested it, makes it cleaner all round to convert to cash and easier for probate."

"I'm sure," said Belinda, "tell me, did any of the film group know about your adoption?"

Tommy shrugged. "They may have or maybe not. I didn't tell them and I don't think Max was interested enough in them to say he had a son. Now, if you'll excuse us, we have a luncheon date." The women stepped back as the engine purred into life and the sleek machine slid gently but swiftly onto the road and passed into the distance.

Hazel joined Belinda as they watched it disappear. "You realise that Tommy had a reason for his adopted father to die," said Belinda, as she began to unravel this new element in the murder of Old Max.

***

Unravelling this new component proved to be difficult and perplexing, and sleep was denied Belinda that night. She glanced at the bedside clock. Nearly 2.00AM. She rose, tiptoed down to the kitchen, made a cup of Camomile tea and settled down before the glowing coals in the living room fireplace. Nothing would remove the thoughts that repeated and repeated in her mind. The police had made no arrest, apart from Harry's charge of unlawful imprisonment and he'd been released on bond. Presumably the police couldn't find any hard evidence against a member of the group or find a hole in their alibis. Or were they biding their time – waiting for the murderer to make a false step? And added to the list of potential murderers, Tommy and Adele; she knew nothing about their movements, but presumably the police were aware now that Tommy inherited the house and where happy with his and Adele's alibi. Then there was Jake's death. Suicide? Or a self-administered overdose? Murder? And if the latter, who gave the fatal injection. And why?

**

Across town in the retirement village a faint light glowed in Lance's window. He too was having difficulty sleeping. The light came from his lap top as he scrolled down page after page. If there was a copy of the missing film, then *he* wanted it. The rest of the group could go hang. But the clues in the VHS tape he stole from Belinda were meagre in the extreme. The only lead was a person by the name of 'Bert' but putting two and two together it seemed likely the film had been copied at a laboratory; but when and where? Max has said thirty of forty years ago. If he could find the names of the film labs in Melbourne at that time, he might be able to find out who the ambiguous 'Bert' was.

He rubbed his eyes, tired from peering at

the computer screen. Standing and stretching he opened the front door and stepped onto the porch. His two cats alerted to the prospect of an unscheduled nocturnal excursion silently padded their way after him. The clouds had cleared and a soft moonlight bathed the roof tops. The air was surprisingly balmy and he took some deep breaths. The shuttered windows of the surrounding cottages appeared as blank eyes that refused to acknowledge his presence. Since his arrest the residents had shunned him, although he noticed a certain widow in the cottage opposite had given him a winsome smile when their paths crossed that morning. Perhaps she sensed danger and toyed with the idea of a fool hardy romance with a 'criminal', as an alternative to the days filled with Bingo and Move It Or Lose It exercises. Lance smiled. No. If he could lay his hands on the film then it would be goodbye to geriatric city; the South of France had always held a fascination for him. The cats' thoughts were more run of the mill – there was something moving in the nearby shrubbery.

***

Another sleepless soul was Harry. Various threads of distrust unravelled in his mind. Why had that lump of lard, Muriel, claim to have seen him and Lance enter the house the day of the murder? Possibly she may have seen him but certainly not with Lance. What was she hoping to achieve by making that statement to the police? So far the cops believed Charmaine when she said she'd been with him all that day, but whether this was a blind in the hope they'd discover his real activities remained to be seen. Lance. What if Muriel was right when she claimed to see him enter the house? Since the funeral, he'd been acting strangely, aggressively, not like his usual insipid self. He'd followed that girl, Belinda, when she disappeared upstairs the day of the wake. The girl had dropped a VHS tape. Did Lance know something about the tape? Was he hiding information from the group, information that related to the missing film? But the negative had been destroyed, so what if...it had been copied onto a VHS tape? No. Not a tape... but a positive print! Had Max made a copy from the negative before it rotted away? A possibility; and also a possibility that Belinda knew about it. As well as Lance? But how to confirm this theory? A visit to troublesome Miss Belinda?

***

"Hello, Muriel. I dropped by to have a chat with Joe." Lance stood at the doorway, a beaming smile on his face.

Muriel wiped her hands on her apron. "You know it was me who told the police you entered Max's house when he was murdered?"

Lance's eyes blazed. For a moment Muriel thought he was going to strike her. "Thank you for telling me that. I'm not likely to forget," said Lance icily, the smile vanishing swiftly. "It caused me all sorts of problems with the cops."

"But I see you're still free."

"Free because I wasn't at the house."

"But I saw you."

"You're lying, Muriel. I don't know why except to divert any suspicion away from yourself."

"Why should I do that? My conscience is clear. I only reported what I saw."

Lance took a deep breath. "Let's stop bickering. For whatever reason, you made the statement which you know is false. The cops have cleared me. Now could we forget that for the moment? I want to see Joe."

"I don't know that I want a murderer in my house."

There was a silence as both looked each other coldly in the eye. Muriel blinked. "Well, you'd best come in. Keeping the door open lets the cold in." So saying, she stood aside to allow Lance to enter. The door firmly shut, she led the way down the hall. "Joe seems to be a popular chap these days, 'someone always wanting to talk to him. Lord knows why."

"Well he knows a lot of film history," said Lance, as he took in the threadbare surroundings.

Muriel gave a grunt either of acknowledgment or disdain. "He's here in his usual spot in front of the telly." She pushed open the door to reveal Joe enthralled in a movie classic. '*Fasten your seatbelts, it's going to be a bumpy night*' rang out shattering the suburban ennui.   Lance entered, and Muriel closed the door on them but stood, her ear pressed against the gap in the door frame. She could only hear muffled voices until the television sound stopped suddenly.

"... and I was wondering if you knew about film laboratories in Melbourne all those years ago, and a bloke called Bert," said Lance.

Joe's reply was faint, but Lance's response was clear. "Oh, so Belinda was asking the same question. Did you tell her?" Deep in thought, Muriel turned and made her way to the kitchen. The lamb stew was bubbling away nicely. Why this interest in film laboratories? She'd have to question Joe more clearly. Before she could conjecture further, Lance called from the hallway, "Muriel, I'm off now."

Muriel hurried to him. "Did you get what you wanted?"

Lance smiled confidently. "Just what I wanted. God bless Joe and his little black book."

"I'd appreciate it if you didn't call here again," said Muriel, "It lowers the tone of the neighbourhood, having murderers visiting."

Lance glared at her. "I think the neighbourhood lost value the day you moved in." He left swiftly with a curt goodbye.

Muriel slammed the door after him but the lock did not catch and she had to slam it a second time. When she returned to Joe, he was flipping through his black book. Muriel took it from his hands and looked at Ann Miller flashing her limbs on the cover. "I think I'll take charge of this."

Lance sat in his car. He gave a grin of satisfaction. Good old Joe. A fountain of information. The laboratory link was tentative, but it was a start. Would he tell the group the priceless film may have been copied? No. He knew that any member who had the information he'd discovered, would have kept it secret in the hope of cashing in on the valuable work of art. Belinda had the head start on him, but with some judicious detective work he could track down Bert Ballard, and once the valuable print of the missing film was in his hands, it would see him strolling the Croisette.

***

"Well, it was just a guess, but I knew he had something on Old Max." Belinda and Hazel looked in dismay at the mugs of instant coffee Sam placed before them. Memories of their previous visit were still vivid in their minds, and Hazel, short of sitting in the street, secured a seat as far from the cat's litter tray as possible. Her eyes scoured the disaster area that Sam called home, but it appeared the animal was out on some nefarious errand. Still, she held the fear it would suddenly materialise beside her, in all its malicious sovereignty.

"You said something the day of the auction, "said Belinda, "something like 'he got what was coming to him', or 'what he wanted'. Who were you talking about? Max? Tommy? I say him, because he inherited the house. And why now, do you say 'he' had something on Max?"

Sam eased himself into his chair, slopping his coffee about as he did so. "Well, I keep my eyes open." To give the lie to this, he closed his eyes and rubbed his brow, spilling more coffee in the process. "A few weeks back, I was at the house, in the bio box doing some repair work on the projector. It's pretty old now and seen better days, so it needs a bit of TLC –"

"Enough with the hieroglyphics," snapped Hazel, her desire for real coffee was becoming urgent, "get on with your story."

Sam opened his eyes and glanced at Hazel. *Yes, just like my ex-wife; silly cow.* He took a sip of what was left of his coffee. "Well, as I said, I was fixing the projector when I heard voices."

"When was this?" asked Belinda.

Again Sam's eyes closed to assist his mental recall. "I'd say it was about a week before Max died –"

"Was murdered," growled Hazel.

Sam was silent for a moment his eyes still closed, but his mind open to suggestions of manslaughter. "*Died*! I went to see who the voices belonged to and Max stormed out of the house followed by Tommy. They were having a screaming argument."

"About what?" said Belinda.

Sam shook his head. "Didn't hear much because they went up the side of the house, but I did hear Max say, 'I never thought you'd turn out like this. Anyway, they'd never believe you.' And Tommy said, 'I can make them believe me. And they're pretty tough on it these days.' Then just as they disappeared up the sideway Max said, 'I don't care, I'll never agree to...' and that's all I heard."

"Agree to what, I wonder," said Belinda.

Sam finally opened his eyes and looked at her. "Who knows, but my guess is that the lad had something on Max and was prepared to use it to get whatever it was he wanted."

"   Blackmail?" said Hazel.

Sam didn't look at her, nodded and said, "Your words not mine."

Armed with this curious new information, and in search of good coffee, Belinda and Hazel stepped out into the alleyway, both deep in thought: Belinda on what they had just heard: Hazel thankful to be out in the open air and away from the odours that prevailed in Sam's abode – grateful also for the absence of that cat. Her thanks were in vain for, at the top of the alley, the cat sat brooding, presenting every quality of a bad-tempered centurion guard.

***

Having dropped Hazel off at the beauty parlour for some heavy-duty maintenance, Belinda stopped her car outside an apartment block in the Docklands overlooking the Yarra River. The newly constructed building still had the brand-new look exclusive to expensive apartments and now joined the other high-rise structures that were dominating the Melbourne skyline. Tracing Tommy and Adele's address had been easy: that fountainhead of information, Bridie, revealed they had taken a serviced apartment until probate was settled when Tommy could finally get his hands on his inheritance. Now, after hearing Sam's story, Belinda was keen to discover more about the couple's past. The story that Tommy had been adopted by Max was a surprise and seemed to be true; he had inherited the house and hence had a reason to see the old man dead. But what of Adele? What was her story?

The lift took her to the top floor, and as Belinda stepped from it, she heard raised voices and a woman scream. Nearing the apartment which Bridie had assured her was Tommy and Adele's, the shouting increased and more screams from a woman. Belinda hesitated at the door. Nearby a cleaning maid emerged from an apartment, her trolley laden with fresh supplies. Belinda turned to her. "What's going on? Should we call the police?"

The maid shrugged. "I wouldn't bother, happens all the time. I think they're a couple of weirdoes. You know. They like it rough, if you know what I mean." With that insight into erotic plasticity, she wheeled the trolley off to refresh another apartment.

Belinda turned back to the door. Should she call the police? Whoever the woman was she was screaming in fear, not delight. Reaching for her phone, she was just punching in 000 when the noise within ceased. Taking advantage of the calm, she rapped loudly on the door. There was a short silence before the door opened. Tommy looked startled to see her and made to block the entrance, but Belinda, with some force, pushed him aside and burst into the room.

Adele was cowering in a corner, and as Belinda stumbled to a stop, she could see the woman had been beaten. A blackened eye and a fresh bloody gash to her forehead was evident. Belinda rushed to her, but Adele backed away. Belinda turned to Tommy. "What are you doing to her?"

Tommy crossed the room and aggressively pushed her away from the wounded woman. "Mind your own business. It's nothing to do with you."

"I'm making it my business," snapped Belinda. She turned back to Adele. "Sweetie, you'd better get to a hospital and have that cut checked."

Adele whimpered and shook her head. "No. I can't leave." She clutched at a blood-drenched handkerchief and tried to stem the blood flow from her forehead.

Belinda looked at Tommy. "If you were any sort of a man you'd take her to a hospital."

Tommy laughed off the suggestion. "What for? She'll get over it. She always does."

"You've done this before? To your wife? Why?"

Tommy shrugged his answer.

Belinda looked at him in disgust. "Well I

think you should let her leave with me so I can get her to hospital."

"She's not going anywhere. Besides, without me, she's got nothing."

"Let Adele make her own decision." Belinda turned to Adele and took her arm. It was then she saw all the bruising. "Sweetie, I want you to come with me, and I'll see that you're looked after. Will you come?"

Adele looked at her with fear in her eyes. "I...I'd like to... but I can't... I don't have anyone... anything..."

"No matter, I'll fix things for you. Trust me."

The distraught woman cast a look to Tommy who stood defiantly with his arms folded across his chest. "I'd like to," whispered Adele.

"Right." Belinda began to move the shivering woman slowly toward the door. Tommy sprang at them, pulled Adele free and pushed Belinda hard against the wall. He raised a hand to strike her.

Swiftly, Belinda grabbed his little finger and his ring finger with one hand while with the other, grabbed his middle finger and index finger. With a hard wrench, she pulled the fingers in opposite directions and bent his wrist away from her. Tommy gave a yelp of pain as his fingers were torn apart. That pain was but a precursor for the agony that was to follow as Belinda brought her knee up and into his family jewels, with enough force to guarantee dislodging several gems. Tommy gave a shriek, double over and fell back on the floor writing in agony.

Wasting no time, Belinda grabbed Adele by the wrist and dragged her out of the apartment and into the foyer. There was an agonising wait for the lift to arrive, accompanied by groans and swearing from the apartment, as Tommy slowly recovered his pride and dignity. Glancing back, the two women saw him stagger into the foyer. Adele gave a cry of fear. As Tommy began a painful move towards them, the lift door opened. Belinda pushed Adele in, and as the doors silently closed, they saw Tommy's face, red with rage, frustration, and pain.

***

"That's was after he adopted Tommy." Adele sat rugged up in a blanket, sipping hot sweet tea, and warming herself by the log fire. Belinda watched the young woman as she shivered not from cold, but from shock. Bringing her to her home seemed the natural thing to do; Adele it appeared, had no one to turn to or anywhere to go, and after what she witnessed earlier Belinda had no plan to see her return to Tommy. So until that could be resolved, she felt responsible for Adele's care.

Hazel, freshly laundered and refreshed by the beautician's skills, added to the balm with a restorative of her own. She took a sip and lowered her glass. "Tell me, how did you and Tommy get together? I understood him to be an orphan."

Adele looked at Hazel over the rim of her

cup. "I was too. Or rather, my father ran away, and my mother couldn't look after me, so I was put in care. That's how we met. Tommy was with a foster family, he'd been with a string of them. Same with me. We met at someone's birthday party when we were about sixteen. He was the only one to show any interest in me, so we became friends and used to hang out together. I guess because we had similar problems and no family to turn to. A real family, I mean."

"Your mother?" said Belinda.

Adele gave a weak smile. "Don't know. She moved away, and I never heard of her again. She could be dead, for all I know – or care."

"Back to Tommy," said Hazel, "what was it about him that attracted you."

Adele put her cup down and wrapped the blanket tighter around her. "He didn't look it, but he was tough and always had a plan to improve things. Like when he got old Max to adopt him."

"Really? How?" said Belinda.

"Well, when they met Tommy could see that the old man took a fancy to him, so he played on that. It started when Tommy used to go to the theatre that Max had. He liked those cheap action films that screened there. He was there so often that Max noticed him and gave him odd jobs around the place. Cleaning up after screenings and that sort of thing. He was invited to Max's house and from then on visited him as often as he could. Took an interest in his films and his history. Made himself useful around the house. Somewhere along the way, he planted the idea of Max adopting him, and the old man fell for it. Made him feel he was doing something good. Liked the idea of having a son."

"Did Tommy know about the film, 'Soldiers of the Cross'?" said Belinda.

Adele gave a half-hearted smile. "He said it was rubbish, and even if it was found any money it made for the group would be peanuts, compared to what he expected."

"So Tommy knew he was to inherit the house and money?"

Adele nodded. "He got what he wanted. But it wasn't soon enough. That's when he went funny."

"How funny," said Hazel.

"That's when he started beating me, and when he..."

"Adele, don't try and protect him now, if he did something else tell us."

The young woman frowned and looked away from them. "Well, at first I thought it was a joke. But then I realised he meant it." She raised her head. "He told Max that he wanted ownership of the house. Now. He wasn't prepared to wait until he died, and if Max didn't agree, he was going to tell the police."

"The police? Had Max done something the police ought to have known about? What?" said Belinda.

Adele gave a sigh and turned to her. "He was going to accuse Max of molesting him when he was young."

Belinda and Hazel exchanged a glance. "And did he? Abuse Tommy?"

Adele shook her head. "No. It was a lie, but he said he was prepared to convince the police it was true unless Max did what he wanted."

"And Max refused?" said Belinda.

Adele reached for her cup. "Could I have another cup, please?"

Belinda poured more tea. Adele snatched up the cup and took a long draught. "If he refused," said Belinda, "Tommy had a reason for Max to be dead. And quickly."

Adele nodded. "I don't think he would have gone to the police and accuse Max. It was just a threat to get what he wanted."

"Very convenient for him when Max was murdered," said Hazel.

Adele looked at her. "I don't want to talk about it." She shivered and once again wrapped the blanket around her as though sealing out the world.

"How did you hear of Jake's murder? You and Tommy were away in the mountains camping at the time.

"The police discovered he was adopted and located Tommy's mobile number. They rang us, and we came straight back to Melbourne."

"And you were away at the time of the murder? Is that right? That's what you told the police, am I right."

Again Adele shook her head. "I don't want to talk about it."

"Why not?" said Belinda. "Is there something you haven't told anyone? The police?"

Adele was silent for a long moment then in a small disappointed voice, "I woke one morning, and Tommy wasn't there. He didn't come back until late afternoon. He'd left me all alone in the bush, and I was scared. Scared of snakes and things. I sat in the tent all day. I was terrified. I asked him where he'd been, and he said it was none of my business."

"Do you remember when this was?"

The woman looked at them with frightened eyes. "It was the day Jake was murdered."

Chapter Fifteen

The glow from the remains of the log fire complemented Hazel's efforts in looking youthful, softening her features so that, should she be able to see herself in this light, she'd never move from the chair. Ever. Fireside contemplation of Adele's revelations had occupied her while Belinda had taken the distressed woman upstairs to sleep and recover her strength. Why a woman stayed with a man when he beat her, was anathema to Hazel, but she understood Adele's claim that she had no one else to turn to but rejected her belief that Tommy would be better when he got what he wanted, which was Max's house and his money.

Amazing how some people can fool themselves. It was clear to Hazel that given the first opportunity, Tommy would dump Adele; she had served her purpose. And the revelation that Tommy was in Melbourne the day Jake died, as well as having a strong motive to kill Max, strengthened the argument he was responsible for both murders. But why kill Jake? What was the connection between them?

These deliberations were broken as Belinda entered and took a seat by the fire. "I finally got her off to sleep. She went on rambling over and over about Tommy and her mixture of love and fear. To calm her down I gave her a sleeping pill, so she should sleep through the night."

"Have you thought what you're going to do with her?" said Hazel.

Belinda grimaced. "Well, we'll have to take her to the police and tell them about Tommy's absence on the day of the murder. She won't like that, but needs must."

"True, but what I meant was, after that. Where will she go? You took her away from the only person she knew, you can't just leave her without any help."

"I know, I know. It's been bothering me too. She can stay here for a while."

"Not long. Aren't your parents due home soon?"

Belinda nodded and sank back into the chair. "In a couple of days. Isn't there some sort of social welfare place for women who have problems?"

"I'm sure there is, but it depends on what the police decide to do with her. They might charge her with withholding evidence."

"They might, but even then they're unlikely to lock her up. What she needs is someone she knows..."

"But she says she knows no one," said Hazel.

Belinda rubbed her brow. "There must be someone who can help."

It wasn't until next morning as Hazel was buttering some toast to take to Adele, who was upstairs in her bedroom, that an answer came. Belinda still in her bathrobe hurried into the kitchen. "Muriel," she said confidently, "Muriel can help."

"What makes you think that," said Hazel.

"Well, she apparently was friendly with Adele and being a nurse –"

"Retired nurse." Hazel wasn't convinced.

"- well alright, a retired nurse, she at least might have some contacts that can help in looking after Adele. She might even take her in."

Hazel looked doubtful. Irritated, Belinda snapped, "Have you got a better idea?"

"No. But don't you think it's a bit – well, dangerous? After all, Muriel is probably still a suspect, as far as the police are concerned."

"But you said she'd dropped off the cake and then went on to a part-time job which no doubt the police have verified. And as I'm the one who took her away from Tommy I feel some responsibility in helping her. Asking help from Muriel, who is one of the few people Adele seems to know, seems logical to me. She doesn't have to take her in if she doesn't want to, but she might provide some answers. Right?"

Hazel still looked sceptical. "I still think you should let the police decide what to do with her, but if you're determined to do it, do it."

"Alright then. It's worth a try. I'll drive over and ask her if she can advise what to do, and ask if she's willing to take Adele in until things get sorted."

Hazel bit into a slice of the toast she had prepared for Adele. "And what am I to do while you're off being Mother Teresa," she munched.

"Take Adele to the police so she can tell them that Tommy may have been in Melbourne the day Max died," said Belinda, as though to a three-year-old.

Slightly miffed, Hazel said, "She's not going to like that. And how are we going to get there? You'll have the car."

"Tram."

"Tram?" Hazel looked surprised and then smiled. "Oh, alright. I quite enjoy Melbourne trams.

***

Hazel was to regret that statement as the tram was crowded, she had to stand, and Adele was a reluctant, sullen nemesis. Being told she must tell the police about Tommy's absence she'd had a screaming fit, refused to get out of bed, eventually flinging a pillow and a plate of toast at Hazel. Enraged, Hazel went into dominant Mother Superior role, dragged the woman from the bed, forced her to dress, pulled her down the stairs into the street and frogmarched her to the tram stop. This had silenced Adele who retreated into a brooding and ominous lethargy.

Struggling through impassive passengers as they arrived at the stop near the police station, with a firm grip on millstone Adele, Hazel stepped from the tram. As she did, she lost her footing, stumbled and clutched at something to prevent a fall.

Two things happened at this moment. Adele took the opportunity to free herself and disappeared into the frenzied passengers crowding to board the tram. In her grasping hand, Hazel made contact with the firm, muscular arm of a young executive; evidence she quickly recognised of his working out at the gym on a regular basis. Dressed in Melbourne Black, he turned curious eyes to her. Eyes she saw that were quite, quite blue and a frisson of lust enclosed her. He had the most captivating smile. She attempted to match her smile to his, but sadly this Adonis deftly removed her talons from his arm, nodded, and boarded the tram. Feeling very much like a shag on a rock, Hazel watched the tram depart, gave a sigh at the loss of a potential strategic manoeuvre, and turned her mind to the realisation Adele had fled – in the middle of the crowded city – and there was little hope of finding her.

***

Belinda turned the car into the street Muriel and Joe lived in. She hadn't paid much attention to it on the previous visit. Located in the inner West of the city the area was in a period of gentrification, but that hadn't reached this street. All the houses had a down at heel look seemingly waiting for developers to either restore or pull them down, to accommodate the towering apartment blocks being constructed to house the mushrooming population. As she parked her car, Belinda reflected on her mission. Was she right in thinking Muriel would help? Take the girl in? And maybe she was dealing with matters that were none of her business. Climbing out of the car she reflected how all this had begun; with the search for a scrap of old film that may or may not exist. She made her way through the run-down garden; grass in need of mowing, the skeletal remains of a few summer flowers, a Lilac bush, a concrete bird-bath bone-dry and sun-baked. Reaching the house, she knocked on the door. While waiting for a response, she glanced around her. The house had seen better days; needed painting, a broken window here and there, and some of the veranda flooring was beginning to rot. It would take some money to bring it up to its former glory, and she wondered if Muriel and Joe were in a position to finance all the work needed.

Clunky footsteps announce the arrival of a resident, and the door groaned open to reveal Muriel's judgmental eyes.

***

Hazel stepped down from Police headquarters. She has delivered the information that Adele had revealed. Revealed also, her stupidity in allowing Adele to escape. The police immediately set out to interview Tommy while at the same time arranging a search of the city streets for Adele.

Weary from the morning's activities she took a seat at an outdoor café and ordered coffee. It was at moments like this she regretted giving up smoking. Her mobile phone rang, and thinking it would be

Belinda, she picked it up. A strange female voice spoke.

"Is that Hazel Whitby?" Without waiting for a reply, the woman continued. "This is nurse Grody from 'Cast Away' Sorrento's Home for the Venerable and Broken Down. I tried ringing your associate, Ms. Belinda Lawrence but she's not answering, so I'm calling you."

Hazel's mind had been occupied with recent events, so it took a moment or two for her to absorb what the woman was saying. "I don't know what you're talking about."

"I'm calling because you were friends with a Mister Bert Ballard."

The memory of the meeting at the nursing home returned to Hazel. "Hardly friends, we just spoke to him one day."

Nurse Grody would not be deterred. "None the less, you left a note with him with you telephone numbers asking him to contact you about his sister's whereabouts."

"But we were told he didn't have a sister," said Hazel, with an acknowledging nod to the waitress who placed a cup of coffee before her.

"That's what we believed," said nurse Grody, "but now that he's gone, the solicitor handling his affairs, advised us he does have one."

"Gone? Gone where?"

"Passed over, dear. Eternal rest."

"Dead? But he said he'd live to be one hundred," said Hazel sounding annoyed.

"They all say that," said this pragmatic angel of mercy, "eternal sleep gets 'em every time. He died a few days ago. Now about this sister. Do you want her address or not?"

Memories again flooded back to Hazel as she recalled Bert saying he believed the missing copy of 'Soldiers of the Cross' might be stored with his sister, Daisy. She rummaged in her bag for a pen, found nothing but grasped a lipstick. Dragging a paper serviette to her, she waited with 'Red Hot Stuff' poised. "Let me have it."

***

Muriel turned to lead the way down the hall. "I'll put the kettle on, and you can tell me what you want." Belinda followed after, struggling to close the door. The hinges were loose, so it was only with difficulty she was able to secure the lock. From the living room came evidence that Joe once again was watching his beloved film classics, or had nodded off and was in a phantom bio box standing between two arc projectors, his eyes fixed on the screen waiting or the cues to appear which meant he was to change from one reel of film to another. The closed door muffled the soundtrack.

'You know how to whistle, don't you? You just put your lips together and blow'.

In the kitchen, Muriel was moving a chopping board bearing diced vegetables and kitchen knife from the table. She looked up as Belinda entered.

"Sit yourself down, dear. Just making a vegetable soup. Joe likes it, and it does him good. Tea alright?" she said, wielding a Brown Betty teapot.

Belinda nodded and took her place at the table. "I've got some news to tell you. About Adele and Tommy."

Muriel paused in spooning tea leaves into the pot. She looked over her shoulder at Belinda. "Oh, yes?" she said cautiously, "and what would that be?"

***

Hazel stopped the waitress as she passed the table. "I need a car. Quickly." The waitress used to foodies in Melbourne making exotics demands shrugged, "Sorry, we don't have any on the menu."

Hazel grimaced in irritation. "Fool. No, I mean I need to hire a car urgently."

"Oh, I see. Let me think." She did so slowly, which caused Hazel's blood pressure to seek a higher plane. "I think... I think there's a car hire place on the next block, next to the 'Heavenly Crumpet' but I wouldn't go there if I was you."

"Why?" said Hazel as she fumbled in her purse to pay the bill. "What's wrong with their cars?"

The girl looked blank. "Cars? No, I meant the 'Heavenly Crumpet'. 'Hellish Stodge' would be a better name."

Hazel was silent, reminding herself that one

shouldn't mock the afflicted. She flung a ten dollar note onto the table and hurried off in the direction of the car hire firm. The waitress pocketed the money and went to tell the proprietor that the 'old bird' had done a runner.

***

"Did he? Well, as for Max's murder I did see Harry and Lance at the house, but I didn't see Tommy." Muriel filled the kettle, put it on the stove and lit the gas. "That's not to say he wasn't there." Belinda had repeated Adele's story that Tommy had been adopted by Max so had a reason to kill him, how he had left her in the bush, alone, on the day that Jake was murdered. "Nevertheless," continued Belinda, "he lied to the police and to us. Hazel has taken Adele to the police this morning, and I'm not sure how they will treat her. Keep her in? Charge her for withholding information? But either way, she's going to need help."

Muriel looked uneasy. "Maybe. Why do you say that?"

"She has no-one to turn to. No family, friends."

"She has a husband, but I suppose if he's a murderer, she may as well be single."

"Not much of a husband," said Belinda, "he's been beating her up."

Muriel raised her eyebrows. "Has he, indeed? That's not good. Looking at him you'd think butter wouldn't melt in his mouth."

"So as it seems the film group is the only friends she has, maybe you could help." Belinda gave a smile which she hoped conveyed enough compassion to weaken any resistance Muriel might make to her plan.

"Help? How?" Muriel sat opposite Belinda and rested her hands on the table. Surprised, Belinda realised how large they were. Weathered. Strong. Like a man's.

Chapter Sixteen

'*After 400 metres turn right into Jocose Terrace then take the second on the left, Possum,*' said Dame Edna. Hazel had fed the address for Daisy Ballard into the car's Sat Nav which was programmed to provide details in different character voices, in this case, The Housewife Superstar. Following the instructions, Hazel was negotiating Melbourne traffic. Heart in mouth, foot trembling near the brakes.

The surprise revelation that Bert Ballard did indeed have a sister and that sister had been located filled Hazel with some excitement. Not that she gave two hoots about the missing historical film but, if found, it would provide some much-needed relief from all the grim hustle of the past few weeks. And it would solve the group's problems - at least financial ones. That is if the sister, Daisy did indeed still hold the print of the film.

'*After two hundred meters enter the roundabout and take the second exit Gay Parade then turn left. Mother used to say there are no strangers, only...*' Muriel missed the rest of the Dame's witticism as she was intent of evading an enfeebled cyclist, a convoy of roaring, noisy bikie gang on hot wheels, an L Plater driving his first car while texting proudly to his mates, and likely to be deceased by teatime. With some relief, she left the roundabout and was proceeding to turn left as instructed. It was then she had a sense of déjà vu; it all seemed familiar.

'Turn left at Acacia Street and you have reached your destination. Spooky, isn't it?'
It was indeed spooky for, as Hazel brought her car to a halt, she realised she was outside the apartment block where Jake had lived - and died.

***

"I agree," said Muriel, "the girl needs help, but what you're suggesting isn't that easy."

"I know I'm making a big ask, but I don't know what else to do," pleaded Belinda.

Muriel rose and poured the boiling water into the pot. She nodded in the direction of the dresser. "Would you get the teacups? They're in the bottom cupboard."

Belinda stood, squatted down and opened a door. A number of metal film tools cascaded onto and around her feet. She winced as a sharp item nicked her ankle. Beyond the tools, she saw a familiar object; a Bourke Street department store bag.

"Oh Muriel, your bulbs. The ones you saved from Max's house." She pulled the large bag out and tipped it over. But no bulbs fell from it. Only a crumpled pinny, stained with dry blood and earth. This was followed by a metal object. Belinda stared at the heavy, tape film splicer, as it clattered to the floor. It had soil clinging to it. She gingerly picked it up by the handle.

Soil, as well as dried blood and matted human hair caught in the blades. In horror, she realised what she was holding.

Eyes wide with shock she looked up to Muriel who was now towering over her. The woman's eyes were cold and hard as steel. She raised a fist.

***

The air was full of dust as Hazel approached the block of flats. Noise and confusion greeted her. Workmen had begun dismantling the old garages, and the garden was littered with fragments of wood and plaster. Old chairs, mattresses, and household items left by deserting tenants added to the turmoil. Holding a handkerchief to her nose, she entered the abandoned building. In the hall, the door to Jake's apartment stood open. It still contained some of his belongings, but scavengers had been in, and the whole place was in disarray. She turned to the door opposite. Number Two. The lair of the cat woman. Was it possible she was Daisy Ballard? And if so, had the missing film been under their noses all the time? Hazel knocked, but there was no answer. Had Daisy moved already? Above the noise of the demolition, she heard the faint wail of a distressed cat. She knocked again, this time thumping the door. A faint "Go away" was her reply. She thumped louder and called, "Daisy? I need to see you." There was a moment, and she heard the door latches being undone. The door opened a fraction, and one of

Daisy's eyes appraised her. "Are you Daisy Ballard? I need to talk to you about your brother, Bert," said Hazel putting a firm hand on the door.

Daisy pulled the door open. "No point. He's dead." She turned and walked back into the room. Hazel followed. "You know?"

Daisy nodded. "Yes, some Collins Street solicitor sent me a letter." She continued with what she had been doing, sorting out clothing. Some she threw into a suitcase, others she dropped on the floor. This was accompanied by the wailing cat now enclosed in a travel basket and clearly in a murderous mood.

"I'm sorry. It must have been a shock," said Hazel

Daisy paused to inspect a grubby bra deliberating on its future. The future was the floor. "Not really. Bert and I haven't seen each other in years. And he was getting on, you know. What do you want? You didn't come to tell me about Bert, I'm sure."

Hazel stepped delicately over a faded pink corset which had seen better days. "Yes, Bert mentioned he had some of his film memorabilia stored here, and I wondered if you still had it."

'Oh yes, all his rubbish. I've thrown a lot of it away, and I'd been meaning to it rid of the rest, but never found the time." She nodded to another room. "It's all in there. When he went into the ga-ga people's home, he dumped them with me. He thought he'd be coming out again." She gave a malicious chuckle. "There's one born every day. You're welcome to take the lot. But be quick about it. I have to be out of here."

Hazel looked at the worn furniture. "But what about your belongings? How are you going to take them?"

Daisy glanced at her. "Belongings?" she snorted, "look around you. Would you want to keep them? No, it's all rubbish. It can join the rest when they knock the place down."

With some trepidation, Hazel stepped over the discarded garments to the other room. It was dark, and she felt for the light switch. "No point trying to use that," said Daisy, "the power's been off for the last week."

Hazel stumbled to the window where a closed blind encouraged darkness. Even as she raised it the dirty window allowed limited vision. She wrinkled her nose at the unmade bed. Nearby, a shabby wardrobe, piles of various magazines reaching almost to the ceiling, a bedside table bearing empty sherry bottles, and a dresser. It was on the dresser, half hidden by a collection of out-of-date pharmaceutical snake-oils, Hazel saw an old magnetic sound recorder, well-worn and torn film magazines, and sealed cans of film. Pushing the medicines aside she removed the cans one by one. Each was labelled, and she squinted to read the faded writing.

Spirit of Progress:
Australia's Wonder Train
1937 Charles Herschell

Olympic Games
Melbourne 1956

His Royal Highness. F. Thring:
George Wallace The Dance of the
Wounded Wombat
as recently performed by the
famous Russian dancer,
Palmolive

Other cans had similar titles. Doubtful now that the missing treasure was within her grasp, she took the last can. The handwritten label was faint and hard to decipher so she moved to the window where, by wiping the glass with a worn pair of bloomers she'd hastily authenticated as clean, the light became a little stronger. Her heart leapt as she began to identify the words.

SOLDIERS
OF THE
CROSS.

Chapter Seventeen

A brilliant flash of light followed by intense darkness embraced Belinda. How long she was unconscious she didn't know, and the first sensation she felt as the blackness receded was a tight feeling across her chest and the inability to move her legs. Twittering sounds close to her ear added to the confusion. She blinked her eyes open. What was this strange place? No... not strange...unfamiliar. Realisation dawned as the mental fog cleared. It was Muriel's kitchen, and the twittering was Muriel muttering to herself. Belinda looked down. Her legs were bound together, and the tightness around her chest was a sturdy rope which tied her to a kitchen chair.

"Ah, you're conscious, good," said Muriel as she tightened the knot on the rope. She moved and stood before Belinda. "The good old Vulcan nerve pinch, or near as damn it. Rather, pressure point knock-out. Stood me in good stead many a time with a difficult patient." She turned and took a small leather bag from a cupboard.

"One swift punch to the neck, strike the vagus nerve, cause false high blood pressure. Your brain tries to lower the pressure, but lowering it just knocks you out." She looked over her shoulder at Belinda. "Just thought you'd like to know." She bent and picked up the metal film splicer and placed it on the table in front of Belinda. "Careless of me not to have cleaned this up and put it back in Max's cinema where it belongs, but you know how things go. Time just got away from me."

Belinda looked at the object in horror. "You killed, Max!"

"Yes," said Muriel impassively.

Belinda struggled against the ropes holding her upper arms firmly against her side. Her hands were free, but she could only pick at the bindings. "Let me go, Muriel. What do you think you're doing?"

"No, I can't let you go, surely you understand that? Silly girl." She turned back to the leather bag and opened it. Belinda strained to see what she was doing. "I'll scream for help. Someone will hear."

"Go for your life darlin', give your lungs some exercise."

Belinda screamed at the top of her voice.

Muriel chuckled. "Waste of breath. All the neighbours are out at work during the day, and I'm sure you don't think Joe is capable of being your hero. He's sure to be asleep or going silly over June Allyson, and when he does that, the rest of the world doesn't exist." She turned to Belinda and placed the items she'd taken from the leather bag on the table. Belinda stared at them in alarm as she realised what Muriel was about to do.

***

Hazel joined Daisy who was trying to cram more clothing into an already overfilled suitcase. "Find anything you like?" said Daisy.

Hazel was picking at the old tape that sealed the can which she now knew contained the missing film. "I think so."

"Do me a favour and sit on this case, will ya?"

Hazel was startled. "What?"

Daisy indicated the suitcase on the table. "Sit on it so I can lock it shut."

Amazed at this request, Hazel put the film can down, and eyed the bulging case. "I'm not sure I –"

"Crap," said Daisy irritably, "just stand on this chair and then you can sit on the lid."

To her amazement Hazel found herself doing what she was told; sitting uncomfortably while Daisy grunted and wheezed as she attempted to get the locks to meet. "You know, when you knocked, I wasn't going to answer the door," she said.

"Oh? Why," muttered Hazel, as the improbability of the situation struck her. Perched on a suitcase on a table in a condemned building. What would her South Kensington friends make of it when she told them – if she told them?

"I thought it might have been her."

"Her? Who, her?"

"The nurse from hell. 'She used to visit that young Jake."

"Was he ill?" said Hazel, squirming to get comfortable.

"Sit still," ordered Daisy. "Ill? If he was, it was of his own making. Sometimes she paid him daily visits.

"Why, 'the nurse from hell'?"

"Let's just say she was no Florence."

"What was she like, this woman?"

Daisy grunted as she succeeded in clicking one lock into place. "Large woman. Always wore a black coat, white smock, and gloves. Black leather gloves. And a funny hat, black as well."

Hazel frowned. "And she saw him regularly?"

"Drugs, dear. Drugs. She supplied him with his drugs."

Startled, Hazel said, "Have you any idea who she was?"

"Not really. I remember Jake mentioned her one day in passing." Daisy took a deep breath and resumed forcing the second lock to meet. "Madelaine...no...Melanie...ah...Muriel. That was it. Nurse Muriel he called her. What with her drugs an' all, I'm willing to bet it was her what gave him his drug overdose. She'd been there that afternoon. I saw her leave. She left Jake's door open so I went over to see him. He was flaked out with the needle still in his arm. I could see he was ill. Dying probably." Shocked, Hazel said in disbelief, "Why didn't you call an ambulance? The police?"

The second lock clicked into place and Daisy stood looking pleased. "Police? Don't be daft. I don't want to have anything to do with them."

With a yelp, Hazel jumped from the table. Belinda was with Muriel at this moment. She had to get to her. Stumbling through the rubbish she ran from the building. Daisy watched in amazement. "You forgot your film," she called. There was no reply. She shrugged and pitched the film can onto the floor with the other rubbish. "Here ya are Bert. A souvenir."

***

The wick flared, spluttered, and burned brightly. Muriel blew out the match and pushed the candle closer to Belinda. "He'd still be alive today if he hadn't been so pig-headed," Muriel said.

Belinda struggled against her bonds. "Shut up and let me go."

Muriel glanced at her. "You know I can't do that, darlin', now be good and keep quiet and let me get on with it." She took a large silver serving spoon from the leather bag and polished it with a cloth. "I only use this for my special customers, so you're in for a treat."
She turned and lit the gas under the kettle again.

Belinda struggled but was unable to loosen the ropes. If she could keep Muriel talking long enough, she might be able to free herself, or someone would come and save her. "Why did you murder Max, why? What had he done to you?"

"He was selfish. He wouldn't give us the missing film. It was valuable, and we could have sold it. Made some money. He had plenty, so he didn't need it."

"Would it have made much difference to you?" Belinda watched in trepidation as Muriel turned back to the leather bag again. "You don't look as though you're short of a penny," Muriel said, withdrawing a clear plastic bag which Belinda could see contained a light beige coloured powder. Muriel continued with some bitterness, "And you've no idea how it is to live on a pension, struggling to make ends meet, and taking on small jobs to stretch the money further. So when I went to tell him how much it meant to me, he called me an old fool. I lost my temper. The splicer was handy, so I used it. Buried it in the garden but I didn't expect the house to be sold so quickly. Had to get it, in case it was discovered."

Belinda wriggled against the rope. It was beginning to loosen. Maybe, just maybe…

Muriel took the kettle and hot water to the table. She tipped a large amount of the power into the spoon. "I don't think we'll bother with accurate measurements today and I usually use a cigarette filter to get rid of impurities, but again, I see no need for that."

Belinda began to perspire as fear overcame her and she watched in horror as Muriel added water to the spoon and held it over the candle flame. "I'm also going to give you another final treat, 'big bertha', a relic from my early days nursing. So much more effective and satisfying than the pissy little needles they use now." She held the needle for Belinda to see. Large, with a robust glass body, and a solid needle equipped with a mind-chilling razor-sharp point.

***

Hazel sped through the streets, with Dame Edna's instructions reduced to incoherent babble. Narrowly avoiding several collisions, she was frustratingly thwarted by a traffic jam caused by an accident. Throwing the car into reverse, she mounted the footpath and, praying there were no pedestrians in her path, bypassed the crowded cars. She was fortunate there were no pedestrians – but there were police who were supervising the traffic. Stunned, they watched as Hazel careered down the path, horn blazing to alert any wayward walker, and turned off at the next corner. Without her knowledge, a policeman and woman raced to their car and gave pursuit.

With a screeching of tyres and then brakes, Hazel pulled up outside Muriel's house. Flinging open the door, she ran into the garden, still oblivious of the wailing police car that screeched to a halt in the street and the two police scrambling out to follow her. She ran to the front door and hammered on it, yelling at the top of her voice, "Belinda! Are you there?" Again she hammered on the frail door. The weak lock gave, and the door flew open. Hazel followed it in a fall but scrambling to her feet she ran into the house calling, "Belinda? Answer me!"

She heard a shriek from the kitchen and pushing aside Joe as he emerged to see what the noise was all about, she reached the kitchen door.

Before her, she saw Belinda tied to the chair with Muriel about to plunge a hypodermic needle into her arm.

Muriel glanced up, paused for a second, then thrust the needle in, pushing the plunger down and delivering the heroin into Belinda's vein.

Hazel rushed forward, glanced down, picked up the tape splicer from the table and flung it with full force at Muriel. It caught her on the side of her head and stunned she collapsed.

Hazel knelt to Belinda whose head sank forward as she went limp. Fearing she was even now too late, and Belinda was already beginning to die from whatever had been injected into her, she frantically began to undo the ropes. She glanced up as the two police entered and showing no surprise at their unexpected presence, barked orders, "Get an ambulance. A paramedic. At once!"

The man turned and began to speak into his phone. The policewoman joined Hazel and felt for Belinda's pulse. "She's barely breathing. What's her name?" she said.

"Belinda," replied Hazel, as she helped to move Belinda from the chair to the floor. The woman began to rub her knuckled fist back and forth on Belinda's chest. "Belinda! Belinda!" she shouted loudly, but there was no response.

Intent on this they failed to see Muriel recover. Ignoring blood flowing from the wound caused by the heavy splicer, she glared at them and hauled herself erect. Grasping the kitchen knife, she raised it and gave a howl filled with hate.

Hazel turned, to see the knife about to be plunged into the policewoman's back. She leapt to her feet and in an untypical move which surprised her - and Muriel - formed a fist and delivered a stinging uppercut to Muriel's substantial jaw. She collapsed unconscious while Hazel, grimacing, rubbed her injured hand.

Chapter Eighteen

"Thank God for Naloxone and paramedics" said Hazel, as she placed a bunch of roses into Belinda's hands. Sitting up in the bed she welcomed her visitor with a smile. The various tubes and hospital paraphernalia attached to her and surrounding her indicated that she was in good hands.

"Yes," said Belinda, inhaling the perfume from the roses, "one of them told me I was very lucky. It blocks the effects of drugs, especially in overdose, which is what Muriel gave me. It worked in about two minutes and got me breathing again, but only last half an hour or so, which means they had to give me more as the effect of the heroin action lasted much longer."

"You look like hell," said Hazel. "That China White was a mixture of heroin and another drug that she pumped into you. How are you feeling?"

"Oh, OK. Still a bit woozy and they want to check me for any damage that might have been done and also to test for any diseases I might have caught from the needle. But tell me, I'm dying to know what happened to Muriel?"

Hazel perched on the side of the bed. "Well, she been charged with murdering Max and denied bail, so they've got her locked up. Mad as a meat axe, to use one of your colloquial expressions.

"Or mad as a cut snake," said Belinda with a laugh. "I'll bet the other members of the group are sighing in relief as they're now off the hook. And what about Jake?"

"Turns out Muriel was a drug dealer. Had her regular customers. It was the job she did to top up her pension. Claimed she did house cleaning but in fact, was known as Nurse Muriel. Jake was one of her customers. She's also confessed to killing him. 'Seems Jake owed her money for his drugs which he couldn't pay. He had to go, so she dispatched him as well. Administered a drug overdose as she was planning to do with you."

Belinda gave a shiver. "Don't remind me?"

"Also, it seems, when she heard he had found the negative and hadn't told anyone, she took vengeance on him, the same reason she did away with Max. Anger, because she wouldn't be getting any money from the sale of the historical film.

"I would have thought she'd be doing alright selling drugs," said Belinda, resettling herself in the bed.

"Apparently not. She wanted to renovate the house for Joe so they would be in comfort."

"Is that all?" said Belinda in amazement. "Two murders out of disappointment and spite." She looked thoughtful. "And I suppose we'll never know what Harry and Charmaine were up to the day of Max's murder."

"Probably better we don't know," said Hazel archly.

"And what about Adele and Tommy?"

Hazel gave a snort. "She's better off without

him. He's been charged with obstruction by the police for lying to them about the day of Jake's murder. Seems he was with another woman who was giving birth to his child. He'd been having a secret affair which Adele knew nothing about. Had several, as it turns out. The police are still looking for Adele."

"Struth," said Belinda, "he's a right piece, isn't he? And you said on the phone you've found the missing film? It was with Jake's neighbour? How extraordinary."

"It seems that way. Turns out she was Bert Ballard's sister. Who knew?"

"That's an amazing coincidence. If you put it in a book, no one would believe it."

Hazel stood up. "Some clever person once said, 'coincidence is God's way of remaining anonymous.' I'd better be off. When will you be free to go home? I'll pick you up."

"Maybe tomorrow. I want to be home before Mum and Dad get back from their cruise. Lord knows how Mum will react when she hears what happened to me. I'll probably be grounded." She smiled at the thought. "Where are you off to?" she asked, as Hazel began to gather her coat and bag.

"Oh, just off," said Hazel, evasively.

"You've got a bloke," Belinda laughed. "Who is it?"

"Well if you must know, he's a cop. The one that called the ambulance for you."

Belinda's eyes opened wide. "But Hazel, he's

a child. A boy. I saw him here at the hospital."

"Well, it's about time he became a man," said Hazel, "and I've got the recipe to make one. Now before I meet him, I'm off to collect the famous 'Sign of the Cross'." She bent and kissed Belinda upon the brow. "Bye," as she walked to the door.

"Wait," called Belinda, "I want to ask you something." Hazel turned. "What?"

"I've been lying here thinking about all that's happened, and one thing keeps bothering me. When we found Jake's body, you said something odd."

"Probably, said Hazel, looking interested.

"You said, 'we have no onions. We have no roast onions."

Hazel frowned. "Roast onions? I don't remember..." Then she smiled and laughed.
"Onions! I read somewhere that in mediaeval times, to make sure someone was dead they applied roasted onion to his nostrils, and if he was alive, he would immediately scratch his nose."

***

Final Curtain

Daisy Ballard shuffled across the now derelict garden, bearing two items; one single suitcase, bulging with her meagre belonging, and the cat in the basket had resumed wailing as it faced an uncertain future.
As did Daisy.

Behind her, the men and machines were at work demolishing the apartments. Walls crumbled, and Jake's apartment was filled with rubble. Across the hall the wrecking ball stunned the foundations of Daisy's home; walls and ceiling folded like tissue paper beneath a torrent of brick and mortar as the whole structure collapsed, burying all the ghosts of people who had lived there over the years; all their activities; their dreams and aspirations; all history was now nothing.

Nothing but a memory.